UNCOMMON STOCK

EXIT STRATEGY

PART III IN THE UNCOMMON SERIES

UNCOMMON STOCK
EXIT STRATEGY

by ELIOT PEPER

Uncommon Stock: Exit Strategy
©2015 Eliot Peper

EDITOR | Shannon Tanner Pallone

ART DIRECTOR | Kevin Barrett Kane

COVER PHOTOGRAPHER | Dane McDonald

THE FRONTISPIECE, INC.
Book Designers

FIRST EDITION.

GET THE INSIDE STORY

To get updates on my new books, reading recommendations, and behind-the-scenes secrets, join my author newsletter. If you love my books, this is the single best way to get or stay in touch with me. Emails are infrequent, personal, and substantive. I respond to every single note from folks on the mailing list. Sign up here:

www.eliotpeper.com

DEDICATION

To Brad Feld, whose encouragement gave me the excuse I needed to believe in myself.

UNCOMMON STOCK
EXIT STRATEGY

1

"AT LAST, the infamous Mara Winkel." Hedrick Verkhov placed a delicate forefinger on his chin and flashed Mara a clandestine smile. "You may be on *Forbes'* 30 Under 30 list, and Mozaik may be the hottest startup in America, but you're sure as hell difficult to track down." He adjusted his signature aquamarine bowtie. "We've wanted to talk to you, here on Hedrick's Report, for quite a while but it took my producers six months to schedule this interview. Are you playing hard to get?"

Mara raised her eyebrows, hoping it wouldn't disturb the makeup artist's painstaking efforts. "The only game we have time for at Mozaik is foosball. We have bigger fish to fry." The heat from the lights was like a tropical sun. It blinded her to the crowd beyond the cameras and turned her nervous sweat into a waterfall. It reminded her of the pivotal DVG press conference, just over a year ago. In reality, she had been thrilled when the producers called. Hedrick was the Jon Stewart of tech, being a guest was an entrepreneurial rite of passage. "But seriously, thanks for having me on the show. Occasionally, we decide to make time for a special someone."

"Aha." Hedrick pressed his hands together and bowed, as if in supplication. "Well, we're honored you're able to be here then." He tapped a pen on the mid-century modern steel desk sprawling between them. The San Francisco skyline twinkled on the wall framing the set. "You mentioned fish waiting to be fried. Not every startup takes down an international bank right after raising their first round of venture capital." Someone out in the audience whooped. "DVG was clearly one of those fish. Who's next? Any stock tips for our viewers?"

Mara pressed her lips together. The rehearsals with the press coach had been key, otherwise she would be seriously flustered right now. "We don't make predictions, we report the facts. And the fact is that everyone has a friend or relative who's been a victim of fraud, even if they haven't gone through it themselves yet." She spread her hands. "Banks and financial institutions experience this problem on a massive scale. Pyramid schemes bankrupt pension funds, leaving beneficiaries destitute. Top executives structure massive embezzlement schemes. Drug cartels find loopholes to clean their dirty money, often collaborating with inside abettors. This is a systemic problem and regulators don't know what to do. They hand down multibillion-dollar fines to banks but the rules are filled with shades of gray and enforcement is an insurmountable challenge."

Hedrick nodded and made a note on one of the many papers scattered in front of him. "Ah, yes. Spell check for financial fraud. But how does Mozaik really work on the inside? What does it actually do?"

Safe territory, back to the scripted answers she had worked on with the coach. "Our algorithms sniff out and flag inconsistencies in financial data. Our analysis highlights suspicious behavior, tracking those dollars through countless shell companies, gaps, and accounts. We're working to drive dirty money out of the global financial system."

"Initiating DVG's collapse certainly qualifies," he said, cocking his head to the side. "You must be making some powerful enemies."

Mara struggled to suppress a shiver. For a moment she wondered whether Hedrick's frank gaze hid some other agenda, whether he knew more than he let on. It made her keenly aware of the absence of the holster at her back. There was simply no way she could have packed heat on *Hedrick's Report*. She reached for the glass of water to cover up her tardy reply.

No. There was no way Hedrick knew about the deaths of Craig, Quinn, and Derrick, or about the truth behind Lars and Maelstrom. She shook herself. This was his job. He interviewed people for a living. She placed the glass back onto its coaster.

"We're making a lot of people nervous," she said, nodding. "Particularly people who are trying to manipulate the financial system to their advantage."

Hedrick raised a finger. "You mean all of Wall Street?"

She laughed. "No, no. We're not after legitimate bankers. We don't make policy or set the agenda. We've simply built a tool that targets *illegal* financial activity. We're looking for money launderers and fraudsters." She didn't add that there were more of those than she ever thought possible. "A healthy financial system means a stronger economy for the rest of us."

Hedrick crossed his legs and swiveled his chair. "But where did this journey start? Was there a garage involved? A magic light bulb going off in your head?" He illustrated the point with a fist bursting into splayed fingers.

Mara's heart rate was beginning to return to normal. Or, at least, national-live-television-broadcast normal. "Garages are so '80s! Now we have coworking spaces." The audience tittered.

Once they settled down, she said, "Actually, I didn't want to get involved in Mozaik in the first place. My best friend, James Chen, pitched me on the idea at the Laughing Goat coffee shop in Boulder. I was doing my undergrad at CU Boulder at the time and I told him he was nuts for dropping out to start a company based on a piece of crazy software. But James is brilliant, he's the smartest person

I've ever met. He soon convinced me that I was nuts to not team up with him. So we made the jump together. Thinking back, it seems like a lifetime ago, even though it's only been a couple years."

"Okay, okay," said Hedrick. "But that's all the public spiel, right?" He pushed his perfectly round glasses up his nose. He was good-looking, in a male model sort of way, Mara decided. But far too aware of it for her taste. Xavier wasn't half as handsome, but he had other talents. Mostly clandestine tradecraft, but would you rather be a talking head or a rolling one?

"Mozaik has been signing up clients like crazy in the year since the DVG blow up. We know you're great at many things. But what do you absolutely, completely suck at?" Hedrick smacked a hand on the desk and the crowd laughed.

She laced her fingers together. The coach hadn't gone over that one. It was hard to internalize that they were speaking to an audience of millions. How were you supposed to gauge your answers? Hopefully, honesty actually was the best policy. "I'm terrible at a lot of things. I forget to call my parents on their birthdays. Sorry, Mom." She gave the camera a quick wave. "I can have a short fuse if something pisses me off. I couldn't write a piece of decent code if my life depended on it."

Hedrick knitted his eyebrows into a frown. "The CEO of a tech company can't write even a line of code?" he asked.

"That's right," she said. "Guilty as charged." She could already imagine how the public relations team was going to harass her over that little revelation. There were probably already a dozen derivative blog posts in the works with click bait titles about how she couldn't program.

"So what do you actually do for Mozaik?" He put both elbows on the desk and leaned forward. "Who's the woman behind the curtain?"

"So far, what has served me as a founder is not discrete skills, but a way of thinking: I am relentless. The work is the work. The path is the path. Ben Horowitz has described entrepreneurship as 'the struggle,' and Paul Graham emphasizes the importance of 'schlepping' to building real value. When I go after something, nothing and nobody will be able to stop me. I once went through thirteen levels of appeal for a $17 parking ticket."

Hedrick chuckled and adjusted his bowtie again. "Seriously?"

"Absolutely," she said. "And that's not all. A few years ago, a friend told me over dinner that they were running a marathon the next morning and joked that I should join. I ran and completed the race in three hours and thirty-two minutes. When I was a kid, I ate corn flakes for every meal for two months despite my parents' constant punishments and cajoling. Now I'm more self-aware of that quality in myself, and it's something I bring to the table every day for Mozaik."

"Remind me not to get in your way." He raised both of his palms. "You certainly haven't let the widely documented sexism and racism in the tech world get in your way. What are your thoughts on inequality in tech?"

The coach had promised her this would come up. No interviewer seemed to be able to resist asking the question. "To be honest, I try not to overthink it. Are there serious gender and racial imbalances in tech? Yes. Is it also a problem in computer science and engineering schools? Of course. Is that also true of other industries? You bet. Does that sometimes result in idiotic behavior from a cohort of repressed brogrammer personalities? Yes. Are inequities real and widespread? Yes. Is this situation ideal? Obviously not."

"Brogrammers, eh?" Hedrick laughed. "I've never thought of Silicon Valley in quite those terms." Damn, more click bait.

"Look," said Mara. "I'm an entrepreneur. I live in the real world and I focus on where I can create an impact. I have a rule: don't work with assholes." Now there was a sentiment she wished she could abide by, even if the producers bleeped it out. "I assume everyone's worthy of my trust and respect when I meet them. But if a colleague mentions my cleavage or makes a disparaging comment because I'm black, I leave the conversation immediately and never interact with them again. Ever. It's just not worth wasting your time on shitty people."

She could thank David for that lesson. If only she could actually follow that advice and cut Lars and his cronies from her life. But Maelstrom's leverage was more than financial. Lars's "care package" swam in front of her eyes, surveillance photos of her friends and family. She coughed to cover the memory of the bald-faced threat. Lars was probably watching this damn interview and it certainly wasn't the time or place for reminiscing.

She looked Hedrick in the eye. "I figure that the single biggest way I can have an impact on gender and racial inequality is by building a company that holds diversity as a core value. And if we succeed, maybe we can be a role model that shows that if the system is broken, then fuck the system. We'll build a new one from scratch."

The audience cheered and she smiled up at them through the onslaught of lights and cameras.

"I see we've got a punk rock CEO on our hands," said Hedrick, grinning. "That sounds like a Burning Man-worthy sentiment."

"We actually recruited one of our VPs at Burning Man," said Mara. "But he's a DJ, not a rock star." Vernon would appreciate the shout-out.

Hedrick reached down, opened a drawer and revealed a slender black and silver axe with a flourish. Mara did all she could to not leap back in surprise. "I've heard you also have a taste for outdoor adventure," said Hedrick with a roguish smile. "This is my lucky ice axe from my climbing days. It's saved my life a number of times and I've kept it nearby ever since."

He laid the axe on the desk and extended his hand. "See that?"

His pinkie finger was missing a joint, a single imperfection in his carefully curated appearance. "Frostbite. To sum up, I was an idiot. But enough about me, what are your favorite ways to get in trouble outside?"

Mara grinned. "We're based in Boulder, so outdoor adventure is in our blood. You should come visit some time. We can take you up to Ouray. When I'm not in the office, my personal obsessions are rock climbing, trail running, and snowboarding. They keep me busy year round."

"Alright," said Hedrick, his expression turning serious again. "From fraudsters to Burning Man to scaling granite cliffs, you've had quite the run so far. What's the biggest challenge you've had to tackle over the past year?"

If only she could tell the truth. "The nature of our work means that I can't share all the juicy operational details. We're taking down financial criminals at a systemic level. These bad bankers enable everything from political corruption to the meth trade. That's a lot to take on! So how do we approach it? We optimize for challenge. We're not comfortable if we're not in over our heads. If things get comfortable, I know we need to reach for new heights. It's not pretty inside the sausage factory but if we do things right, your bratwurst will be mouth-watering." She winked.

"Ladies and gentlemen," said Hedrick, raising his hands to the crowd. "High finance, bleeding edge technology, binary, bad guys, and bratwursts. You definitely want to be on Mara Winkel's good side." He turned to her. "Thanks so much for coming on the show."

"Thank you," she said. "It's been an honor." They shook hands. She knew the entire team back in Boulder would be watching, conference tables loaded with exotic popcorn from Terra Thai.

"Good luck," he said, as applause washed over them.

"Oh, I'll need it," she said. More than he could know.

2

"Sue's already giving me shit about the 'don't work with assholes' line," said James, the exasperation obvious in his voice even over the phone.

Mara laughed. "I figured as much. Just blame it on me."

"Yeah, yeah. Doesn't stop her though."

"It better not." Mara took a sip of her cappuccino. The new breed of San Francisco coffee houses featured roasts far too light and acidic for her tastes. For a moment she yearned for the dark, thick brews of the Laughing Goat. "We hired her to be a PR bulldog. If she's not chafing at the bit, that's when I get worried."

"I think she was expecting worse, she gave up pretty quick."

Mara grinned despite herself. It was good to be working so closely with James. It felt like when they were rewriting the original business plan over a crumb-laden coffee table. If you were going to go through the ringer with someone, it might as well be your best friend.

"Well, I'm happy to hear it wasn't a complete flop," she said.

"For what it's worth, we've had an enormous spike of general traffic."

"Yeah, and my inbox is full of reporters and bloggers. I just forwarded them to Sue. Let her deal with 'em."

"That's the spirit."

"Hopefully this attention will convert into even more paying clients."

"Not too fast," said James. "We're having trouble just keeping up with the current case load."

"I know, but these are still early days," said Mara. A man stepped through the doors into the café. She recognized Fred Bernum from the profile picture Vernon had showed her. He was a hulking blonde who looked like he could have been a Viking if he hadn't gone into banking. "Speaking of ¾ there's my guy. Gotta' run. I'll be back in Boulder this afternoon."

She signed off and dropped the phone into her purse, waving Fred over. They shook hands and he sat across from her. She had been lucky to secure this small table in the corner of the coffee shop. Two chairs and far enough from the baristas to have a conversation without being interrupted by the hissing espresso machine.

Fred was wearing a tailored suit and pointy leather shoes. The wealth suggested by the outfit clashed with the poverty of the panhandler who had been sitting on the sidewalk as she stepped into the café. San Francisco was a city of contrasts.

"Look," he said, crossing his arms. "I'll get straight to it. We're interested in what you're doing at Mozaik, but we're concerned about blowback." His voice was high and a little reedy. It didn't match his body.

Mara nodded and pursed her lips. "We get that question a lot, as you can probably imagine."

"Obviously, I'm not saying we're anything like DVG." He uncrossed his arms and held up his hands. "But our management team doesn't want to expose the bank to any undue risk factors." Fred was the Director of Partnerships for Crutch & Lansum, a San Francisco-based commercial bank.

Mara nodded and sipped the cappuccino. "Risk is a funny thing," said Mara. "It can't be prevented, only managed. Mozaik will change Crutch's risk profile. Yes, you may discover that your accounts need some spring cleaning. On the other hand, if you're blissfully unaware of someone perpetrating fraud within the firm, it will come out eventually. And when it does, ignorance is not a viable defense. What poses a larger risk than that?"

"We don't have anything to hide." He snorted.

"Look Fred, despite what you may think, I'm not here to sell you. We have more work than we can handle with seventeen major banking clients and more analyses coming online every day. Yes, DVG collapsed. But they were up to their necks in fraud at the highest level. That's not every bank. We wouldn't have customers if we sent them directly to the gallows. Our priority is helping you to run a clean ship, not annihilating you."

She drained the last of her cappuccino. He was nodding slowly, tapping a thick finger on his thigh.

"If you're not interested, that's fine," she said. That was the benefit of everyone always asking the same question, you got a lot of practice refining the answer. "We'll be working with your forward-looking competitors to ensure their books are as spotless as everyone likes to claim. Crutch is free to rely on hope instead of data science."

She pushed back from the table and stood. "I've got a plane to catch," she said. "If you change your mind, Vernon can schedule a feasibility study and get the ball rolling."

The bell tinkled as she stepped through the swinging door onto the street. She dropped a few dollar bills into the battered fedora sitting in front of the grizzled panhandler. Crutch would come around. Fred's pushback had been mild compared to what the other banks were saying.

She'd be willing to bet he'd be calling Vernon within the next two weeks. The real trick was going to be fitting them into the release pipeline. It would mean hiring another two statisticians and three engineers. Plus, a dedicated account manager to keep Fred happy. Ramping up new people had proven to be the limiting factor. Mad dash had somehow become the de facto pace at Mozaik.

Her phone buzzed as she made her way through San Francisco's Financial District toward Montgomery BART station. She stopped short as she saw a text from Juliana Estevez.

Mara grinned, remembering the first time she had met Juliana at her office in New York. The woman was a battle-axe and DVG had discovered to its dismay that blades that sharp cut both ways. Initiating the immolation of her employer had blacklisted her for a job at any bank on Earth. But in response to the public outcry against Wall Street excess, the President herself had brought Juliana on as financial reform czar. Mara hadn't talked to Juliana in months.

"Can you be in D.C. on Friday? It'll be worth it. I promise."

3

———————

EARLY MORNING SUNLIGHT FILTERED through the window. Mara blinked slowly and rubbed the sleep from her eyes. Yawning, she arched her back and stretched. If only she could actually get eight hours in every night.

She felt movement on the bed behind her and rolled over. Xavier had kicked off most of the blankets and was on his back, snoring gently. The light from the window played over the scars etched into his chest. She brushed them with her fingertips, feeling his diaphragm expand and contract with each breath. Resting her chin on his chest, her fingers moved down over his stomach to burn and bullet marks on his right thigh.

No hair had regrown over the splotchy scar tissue the boiling oil had left in its wake. The bullet had left a crater at the center of the burns. The skin felt smooth and tight under her fingers.

"Admiring your handiwork?"

She looked up at him. Xavier's head was propped up on the pillow, gray eyes open.

"You deserved it," she said, squinting at him.

He grinned. "Fair enough," he said. "It hurt like a bitch, I can tell you that much. But even so, you looked damn sexy standing there in the doorway, naked with a gun in one hand and a smoking cast iron pan in the other." He ran a hand through her hair. "It was straight out of a Tarantino movie."

"I did go Kill Bill on your ass," she said. "Be careful whom you try to manipulate."

"Manipulation is 99 percent of my job," he said. "I've never been ambushed like that by an agent though."

"I'm not your agent. You're not my case officer."

"Right. And I'm not your agent and you're not my case officer either. Call it what you want, we're helping each other out."

They were quiet for a moment. Birds chirped outside the window, and a garbage truck rumbled up the street, clanking and banging like an urban dragon as it consumed the contents of a dumpster.

She had originally been attracted to Xavier because spending time with him felt like an escape to normalcy from a world gone insane. Now it felt like he was the only person that she could actually be honest with about that insanity. His profession was already a part of the shadows. Conspiracies like Maelstrom were targets to him, not paranoid delusions. Telling him the truth didn't endanger him any more than he already was. He would sometimes disappear for days or weeks at a time, completely off-grid on an operation. But that was fine with her. They would never have a real relationship but the occasional hookup was a fun way to let off steam.

She sighed. "Dear Abby, I'm sleeping with a spy whom I assaulted with a deadly weapon when he tried to recruit me as an agent. Now we're working together to take down a cabal of international criminal masterminds. What should I get him for his birthday?"

"Macallan, 25 year," he said. The lines around the edges of his eyes crinkled. "Duh."

She laughed.

"I've always found reality to be far stranger than fiction," he said. "Imagination is as much our downfall as our salvation. You know, I once investigated a guy working on re-engineering new gene therapies into individually targeted bio-weapons. He was trying to make poisons that would only work on specific people. He financed the entire operation from the proceeds of a smuggling operation that brought Canadian maple syrup across the border into Vermont. That's how we ended up catching him. Pitch that to a Hollywood producer and they'll tell you the audience won't buy it."

"Maple syrup, eh? I guess we're in the wrong business with the whole finance angle."

"I'd say Mozaik is doing just fine."

"Except for the fact that we have a money laundering kingpin on our Board, and at least three people have died already." The air in the room suddenly felt stale and oppressive. She needed to get moving.

"There's that," he said. His expression sobered. "Don't worry, Mara. We will take down Lars. But we need to do it right, and that takes time."

"Time, time, time," she said, sitting up on the edge of the bed. "Speaking of, I'm already running late for my flight to D.C. Give me a ride to the airport?"

4

DÉJÀ VU CLUNG to Mara like the emotional hangover of a forgotten dream. A veritable library on financial ethics lined the walls of the office. An old framed copy of the Constitution hung behind a plain wooden desk with a workstation and a legal pad. The faint smell of sage teased Mara's nose. The only hint to the fact that she was sitting in the White House was the ornate scrollwork framing the window.

Hearing the door open, Mara stood and turned.

"Mara, so good to see you," said Juliana. The streaks of gray in her hair were new, and matched her conservative suit. Beyond that, she looked almost exactly the same as when Mara had last seen her nine months before.

Mara stepped forward and they shook hands. "Juliana, good to see you. It's been too long."

"It has indeed." They sat with the desk between them. "Welcome to Washington."

"I had to go through about fifteen different security checks," said Mara, raising an eyebrow. It had taken forty minutes to finally get in, like airport TSA on steroids.

"Yes." Juliana snorted. "Working at the White House isn't all it's made out to be. *House of Cards* and *The West Wing* are packed with intrigue and excitement. The reality is much more...bureaucratic.

Process and paperwork, the bread and butter of policymaking."

"Sounds like a nightmare," said Mara.

"Kafka would love it," said Juliana.

"I've got to tell you," said Mara, waving a hand to encompass the office, "I almost thought I had been teleported back to your old office at DVG in New York. Did you bring the Constitution with you when you left?"

Juliana made a face like she tasted something bitter. "There was no way I was going to leave it in their dirty hands. They had done quite enough damage already."

Mara sobered. "True enough."

Silence hung in the air for a moment. Mara remembered the backstage room before the big DVG announcement last year. She had been so nervous and pumped up. They had thrown the dice without any idea where they might land. That was the first and only time she had seen Juliana look vulnerable.

"So how do you like working for Uncle Sam again?" asked Mara.

Juliana shook her head, returning from reverie. "It's fine. Not enough resources. Not enough staff. Not enough progress. Lobbyists for the financial industry have big budgets, which mean big campaign dollars. Big campaign dollars mean serious political opposition to most efforts at reform. Pretty much what I expected." She shrugged. "How are things at Mozaik?"

"Intense," said Mara. "We're chasing demand right now, trying to ramp up people and resources fast enough to keep up with customer requests. How many people did we have when you were in Boulder?"

"Around fifteen."

"Right," said Mara. Her mind shied away from thinking about the sheer volume of work they had slogged through in the past twelve months. "Now we have almost two hundred and we're on track to bring in thirty five million in revenue this year."

Juliana froze. The lines on her face etched texture into what would make for a beautiful still life portrait. Her mouth worked for a moment.

"Mara," said Juliana, voice husky. "I knew Mozaik was doing well but, my God, that's simply incredible."

Mara nodded. "And so much of it is thanks to you. Without your courage, we never would have had such a dramatic kick start in going to market." If only they could have taken Lars down in the process instead of getting played by him.

Juliana picked up the pen from the legal pad, put it down again. "You handed me the weapon I needed. All I had to do was use it."

"And put yourself and your career at risk by doing so."

Juliana waved the comment away. "That job was already eating away at me from the inside out. I wouldn't have lasted." She extended both hands, palms up and made a show of looking around the room. "The American taxpayer, or at least their elected executive, has been kind enough to offer me employment again."

A flock of starlings flitted past the window, dark against the blues and grays of the sky beyond them.

Mara leaned back in her chair. "Look, Juliana. Don't get me wrong, it's wonderful to see you again." She pursed her lips. "But I was in San Francisco on Wednesday, Boulder yesterday, and now I'm here. I nuked my schedule to make this happen, and I'd do it again in a minute, given our history. But I can't imagine you asked me to come to Washington, on such short notice, just to catch up. What's so important that you needed to see me so urgently?"

"Have you been following the American STEM Education Act?"

Mara shook her head. Where was this going?

"Congress passed it this week."

"Juliana, can you cut to the chase?" Mara shrugged. "What does this have to do with me or Mozaik?"

Juliana stood. "Let's take a walk."

5

"THE AMERICAN STEM EDUCATION ACT provides funding for all qualified K-12 programs in low income schools around the country. It also authorizes more spending on scientific basic research programs, and provides federal student debt relief for college students studying engineering and the hard sciences," said Juliana. "The President is going to sign it right there next week."

Juliana pointed ahead across the painstakingly manicured lawn to the stairs leading up to the white colonnade and long windows of the Oval Office. Bees were hard at work on the hundreds of multi-colored roses in the beds around them. Low boxwood hedges surrounded the flowers and crabapple trees rose above them, gnarled and lush.

Mara made a conscious effort not to clench her fists as they ambled over the grass. "That's great. There's a technical talent vacuum out there right now. We're competing with the biggest tech companies out there for the best developers. It would be great to have more high-skilled graduates to hire. I'm glad to hear the government is taking an interest."

"Do you know what a rider is?" Juliana gave her a sidelong glance.

Mara thrust her hands into her pockets. "Nope."

"It's an example of what's become the ugly norm for getting things done on the Hill. Essentially a rider is a non-germane amendment added to a bill to serve some kind of special interest. Think corporate tax loopholes baked into an immigration bill or something."

"Okay," said Mara. She was starting to sweat under her blouse. It was early fall but the D.C. sun hadn't lost its summer swelter.

"Like most bills these days, the American STEM Education Act is a Frankenstein. Congress just stitched together a quilt of riders and passed the damn thing wholesale."

Juliana shrugged and continued, "Normally, I'd be appalled. It's a crass and opaque way to make policy. But it's the reality of doing business here these days."

Mara looked up. High altitude clouds skittered across the sky. "Are you saying we need to start hiring lobbyists?"

"What?" Juliana looked genuinely surprised. "God, no. I'm telling you that I hitched a rider onto the STEM Act."

"I thought you just said they were 'crass and opaque.'" Mara bookended the phrase with finger quotes.

Juliana sighed. "I guess my foray into the private sector made me more pragmatic."

Mara raised her eyebrows. "So, what inspired this illicit burst of practicality?"

She had meant the comment to be a joke but Juliana's expression turned serious. The older woman stopped on the grass and turned to face her. The sunlight highlighted new lines around her eyes and the brightly colored flowers all around them belied the gravity of her gaze.

"You," said Juliana.

6

MARA SIPPED ON THE CAPPUCCINO FOAM and looked around the Batcave conference room. Stalactites hung from the ceiling, tastefully integrated to make the light appear to filter through subterranean shafts to the outdoors. The walls were textured like an underground cavern and the Bat-Signal design was engraved in the center of the table.

In the mad scramble of the past year, they had taken over their entire office building in downtown Boulder. Every kitchen had a treasure trove of exotic teas to delight any connoisseur and every conference room had a superhero theme. James's favorite was the Fortress of Solitude but Mara was partial to the Batcave, and she had called this meeting.

The door opened and in filed her core management team. James had a severe case of bed head and a t-shirt that said, "In the beginning... was the command line." Vernon sported a pink polo over khakis, and Gordon's pear-shaped body appeared to be more determined than ever to escape the confines of his ill-fitting button up. She gave each of them a hug, holding her breath to avoid the citrusy scent of Gordon's too-strong cologne.

They all found seats around the conference table.

She couldn't stop herself, she laughed. It really was hard to believe.

"What?" asked Vernon, looking at her quizzically. He now wore his dark hair longer than when Mara had first met him at TechPitch in San Diego. It made him look older, more sophisticated.

"It's just difficult to imagine that the four of us are in charge of keeping this ship on course," she said. "I mean, look at us." She gestured around the table. "Ragtag would be generous, am I right?"

Gordon snorted. "You got that right. I just count my lucky stars that we aren't having problems making payroll."

Vernon made a face at him. "Only you could make Mozaik's success so far sound dire."

"I'm just saying," said Gordon. "We're doing well but we're burning funds fast too. Even companies with solid contracts in place hit cash flow problems."

"We may look ragtag." James smiled. "But first impressions can be deceiving."

"The team at DVG looked slick," Vernon raised an eyebrow. "I hope that's serving them well in federal prison."

"True enough," said Mara, nodding.

James swiped the jet-black hair hanging over his face. His glasses were different. The thin rectangular frames made him look older, almost scholarly.

"So," said James. "We're all happy to have you back in Boulder, Mara. But do we really need to meet on Saturday morning? I'm guessing there must be something unusual going on, what's the big deal?" He leaned back in his chair

Mara put both hands on the table. "Don't worry, guys. This is worth it. Thanks for coming in."

She took a deep breath, savoring the moment. "As you know, yesterday I met with Juliana in Washington. After DVG wound down, she was recruited to be the Administration's new financial reform czar." The sweetness of the roses had blended with the scent of freshly cut grass. She still couldn't believe this was happening. No matter how much planning you did, new variables always seemed to find a way into the game.

"We know that much already," said Vernon, fiddling with the collar of his polo.

"What you don't know," said Mara, "is that she's issued us a challenge."

7

MARA GRINNED. "Juliana added an Easter egg to the American STEM Education Act, a bill that Congress passed earlier this week. It establishes a concrete set of fraud compliance guidelines for financial institutions. Basically, if banks implement software systems that perform according to a set of specifications, they are considered in compliance with federal regulation and will not be held liable for future breaches."

Vernon and Gordon both frowned. James looked back and forth between them.

"That sounds like something I might hear on C-SPAN," he said. "Can you please translate it into plain English?"

"Wait," said Vernon. "What are the specifications the software has to meet in order to establish compliance?"

Mara's grin widened. She had never expected to receive this kind of gift on her trip to D.C. "The specs are based on Mozaik's architecture. Juliana essentially created them by describing what our algorithms already do. She saw what we could accomplish at DVG and transformed it into a federal mandate."

"Holy shit," said Vernon. "Holy fucking shit."

"Bingo," said Mara.

James raised his hands. "If someone doesn't explain what the hell is going on, I'm going back to bed."

"James," said Mara, biting her lip, "Juliana just handed us a monopoly on a silver platter."

"But why would the banks agree to this?" asked James. "Wouldn't it mean the government is telling them how to run their own financial security systems?"

"That was my first question too," said Mara. "But the banks clamored for it as soon as Juliana floated the idea with their representatives."

"Hah," said Vernon. "It's their get-out-of-jail-free card, isn't it?"

"That's right," said Mara. "For banks, the most unmanageable thing about anti-money laundering and fraud laws is uncertainty and liability. The government says that banks must operate according to all laws and regulations, in good faith. If there's a breach, and the bank is found to not have been operating in good faith, it often results in billions of dollars worth of fines."

"What constitutes good faith?" asked James.

"That's just it," said Mara. "There are no clear guidelines for internal enforcement mechanisms. A gray area that costs banks billions in fines, legal fees, enforcement investments, you name it."

"So by implementing Mozaik, or something like it," said James, "they've now eliminated their exposure to that risk and uncertainty because the government won't hold them liable if something goes wrong?"

"Eureka," said Mara. "We're their insurance policy. And correct me if I'm wrong, but there's nothing like Mozaik out there right now."

"Hence, the monopoly," said Vernon. "But won't that just drive malfeasance overseas? Dirty capital flight?"

Mara clapped her hands. "All banks that want to do business in dollars have to abide by American financial law. Mozaik is going to be the standard anti-fraud protocol for the entire global banking system."

They all sat in stunned silence for a moment.

"Fuck," said Gordon.

"What?" asked Mara.

"I just lost my job," he said.

The others all exchanged looks. Gordon shook his head, despondent.

"What are you talking about?" asked James.

Gordon snorted, the sound rumbling up from deep in his throat. "Mozaik has 197 employees and a small client base of banks. James, how many new developers will we need to service the entire international financial system?"

James squinted. "Hundreds."

Gordon nodded and turned to Vernon. "How many new folks will we need working on the business and partnerships side?"

"Hundreds more," said Vernon, pursing his lips.

"Mara, —"

"We get the idea," said Mara. "What are you getting at?"

Gordon raised his eyebrows and leaned back, the chair creaking underneath him. "Getting to that scale that quickly means we're going to have to capitalize this company up the wazoo. We'll have to hire an army and buy out complementary businesses to staff up." He threw his hands in the air, taking in the stalactites. "And unless any of you have a Bruce-Wayne-worthy trust fund to draw on, the only way to do that is to take Mozaik public."

8

JAMES PUT A HAND on Mara's shoulder as the others filed out of the conference room. He held up his phone and raised his eyebrows, then placed it on the conference table. Mara took the hint and did the same with her phone.

"Let's take a walk," he said.

They took the stairs down to the lobby and exited onto Walnut Street. It was a beautiful late summer morning. Joggers were out in force, dodging around the bubbly brunch crowd.

They walked the two blocks over to the grassy open space abutting Boulder Creek. Mara remembered her first visit to CU Boulder when she had been a prospective student. Her parents had come along for the trip and after the obligatory orientation sessions, they had wandered the campus and the town. She had been amazed by the green spaces that sprouted up every few blocks in this little corner of Colorado, very different from the concrete jungle of L.A.

"When's the next board meeting?" asked James.

Mara shook her head, returning to the present. "The week after next," she said. "Wednesday." In the madness of the last week, she had forgotten all about it. There was a lot of preparation to do. She sent out all her updates in advance now. That way the meetings themselves were focused on strategic discussion instead of content delivery. That had shortened the meetings dramatically, especially because neither David nor Lars seemed to enjoy each other's company. Before this week, there had already been substantial material for board review. Juliana's revelation eclipsed all that.

James twitched his nose to push his glasses up. "And how do you think Lars is going to react to this news?" Behind the glasses, Mara could see concern in his eyes.

It was a very good question. She had been so concerned with thinking about repercussions for the company that she hadn't yet devoted much time to considering how Lars and the rest of the Board would respond to the news.

"To be perfectly honest, I don't know," she said. "From the purely business perspective, he should theoretically be thrilled. If we go public, he'll have the opportunity to sell his shares in Mozaik to public market investors for a high multiple. That's why any VC would be excited by one of their portfolio companies going public."

"Okay. But does he want to sell his shares and get out?" His tone implied it would be too good to be true.

Mara shook her head. "I doubt it," she said. After the DVG scandal, Lars had left Mozaik pretty much alone. He had participated in quarterly board meetings and had requested in-depth technical updates from James, but that was about it. They kept waiting for the other shoe to drop.

Mara's fists tightened as she remembered getting in the back seat of the SUV with him. That had been seriously stupid. At the time she had been so overwhelmed from the big press conference that she hadn't been thinking straight. She would never let anything like that happen again.

"The last time Lars talked to me one-on-one, he said that he would be getting more directly involved," she said. "He said he didn't want to play games anymore and would be giving us explicit instructions and expecting us to follow them to the letter."

"So why hasn't he?" asked James.

"Maybe he hasn't needed to yet," she said.

They paused in the middle of the bridge. Leaning on the railing, they watched the creek tumble by underneath them. The water churned and eddied around rocks and roots. She could almost imagine they were somewhere in the mountains instead of in the middle of town.

"If I were Lars," said Mara, "maybe I wouldn't want Mozaik to go public. If we go public then the visibility and transparency of the company both go way up. We're going to have new financial reporting requirements, more formal governance, and a lot more oversight from the SEC. If he wants to play puppeteer, it's going to make his life harder."

James chewed his lip. "And if he doesn't want us to go public, what are our options?"

Mara shrugged. "Gordon is right, we'll need a truckload of cash to be able to service the clients that Juliana just handed us. I guess we would need to raise another round of private financing. Another fund would need to invest a big chunk of dough so that we can scale up."

"You are coming to dinner tonight, right?" asked James.

Mara frowned at the non sequitur. "For the last time, yes," she said. "Don't worry, we're triple confirmed."

James nodded. He looked preoccupied.

"I just hope we're not pissing Lars off," he said. His head sunk between his shoulders. "We've already put so many people at risk. I think about it whenever I'm with Danielle."

Mara put her arm around his shoulder and pulled him close. They stood together looking at the water swirl beneath them, a few dried leaves floating like wild kayakers along the churning currents. Sunlight danced on the surface, highlighting the fractal edges of the ferns dangling their fronds over creek.

Nausea had hounded her for hours after she had opened the

care package of surveillance photos last year. Knowing that Lars had people watching their closest friends and family was sickening. And she had seen the lethal retribution of his methods up close. A steaming pool of blood on the black asphalt was all that had been left of Quinn within five minutes of the ambush. To his credit, that's all there had been left of Dominic too.

"I know." Her voice was almost too quiet to hear. "But the only way out is forward." If only she could be so sure.

9

MARA, JAMES, AND DANIELLE sat on cushions and ate off of the coffee table in James's apartment. Since Danielle had moved in, James had turned into something of a homemaker. His once grungy windows were now scrubbed clean. The abandoned bowls of ramen were conspicuously absent. He had prepared the plates of food on the table from scratch.

"I love this stuff, it's like Asian ceviche." Danielle held up a fork loaded with chunks of fresh fish, chili, onion, garlic, and green pepper. She really pulled off the librarian look. Square rimmed glasses framed the most intense gaze Mara had ever encountered. A chaotic pile of frizzy brown hair and loose teal sweater completed the picture. James had been right, they had grown on each other and Danielle had become one of the most trusted members of Mozaik's core team. Still no sense of humor though.

"Yeah, my aunt was from the Visayas in the Philippines," said James, swiping away his hair and shoveling in a big mouth full. "She used to make *kinilaw* all the time. It's marinated in lemon juice and coconut vinegar."

"It's delicious," said Mara with conviction. The dish was the gastronomic equivalent watching a big budget action movie in 3D IMAX. So many powerful flavors careened off each other and then somehow came together into a delectable finish.

The conversation meandered along familiar lines. Gossip over about the new hires, frustrations with the internal project lead at Bank of America, a new single source Oolong tea that James had recently discovered. Mara settled into the comfortable back-and-forth, letting the diverse spices dance and sparkle on her tongue.

"So how are we dealing with security now that you're deploying code in live banking servers?" Fred from Crutch & Lansum had been hounding her and Vernon with follow up questions about Mozaik's security architecture.

James made a face and took a sip of Pinot Gris. "It's like playing Jenga with a bunch of preschoolers." He looked at Danielle. "Care to explain?"

"If I must." She wiped the corner of her mouth with her napkin. "Banks have many layers of proprietary security software that's supposed to insulate them from malware. It's a nightmare to deal with, we're way more secure than them."

"Wait," said Mara. "Why are we more secure than them if they have all this security software protecting them?"

Danielle loaded more food onto her plate. "The short version is that when you lay good code on top of bad code, the result is still bad code."

"Well said," said James.

"But why is their code so bad?" asked Mara. "They must be spending a lot of money to keep their systems safe."

Danielle nodded. "They're definitely spending a lot of money," she said. "But most of it is counterproductive. The fundamental problem with computer security is that proprietary software has an inherent weakness. If your code is closed, and someone discovers a bug, then it's easy to exploit. That's why Linux works so well. It's open source. The code is available to everyone for free. That means that thousands of people have combed through it countless times and helped each other to fix bugs and close holes. But financial software is different. Banking systems run on proprietary software. Proprietary software is owned and controlled by the company that develops it. That company tries to find and eliminate problems. They even hire white hat hackers to search for new exploits. But at the end of the day, any proprietary piece of code is far weaker than its open source equivalent. And banks mash so many pieces of proprietary software together that the result is a very leaky bucket if you know where to look."

"And that," said James, "is why I'm always pushing for us to release more of our code to the open source community."

Mara raised her wine glass. "And that is where I always push back. There's a good reason so much banking software is proprietary, although you may not like it," she said. "If we open sourced Mozaik's algorithms, anyone could use our code for themselves. Banks could implement everything internally the next day. Consulting firms could implement it. Other software companies could modify it, add to it, and never pay us a penny. You can't charge for open source software. It's like an author publishing her novel on a blog for anyone to read, copy, and share. Sure, people might recommend edits and add missing commas. But who's going to buy her book when the story is available for free?"

"What about Red Hat?" asked James.

"Yeah," said Danielle. "They're successful and they support Linux."

"Sure," said Mara. "And how many other companies have succeeded with that business model? And how many new products has Red Hat been able to invest in and develop? If all you do is maintenance and support for an open source project, you just can't capture enough of the value you're creating to build a real company around it."

"We've been over this territory before," said James with a theatrical sigh.

Mara nodded and laughed. "Luckily, I have you two to keep me grounded on how shit actually works," said Mara.

James raised his glass. "And luckily, we've got you to keep us grounded in what's commercially viable," he said. "Yin, yang, and all that jazz."

They clinked glasses and finished the last of the Pinot Gris.

James disappeared into the kitchen to grab something from the fridge. He raised his voice so that they could hear him. "But we didn't invite you over just to debate philosophies of software architecture," he said.

Mara looked at Danielle who couldn't repress a wide grin.

"What is it?" asked Mara.

James returned to the living room with three flutes in one hand and a bottle of champagne in the other.

"Danielle and I got engaged," he said with a smile as bright as a spotlight.

"*What?*" A rush of warm rose up inside Mara. "Are you serious?"

Danielle flushed. "When we got home yesterday, every single device started to go off at the same time. My phone, my laptop, everything was beeping and going nuts. I thought I had been hit by a nasty virus. But when I opened them, James had simultaneously sent a picture of us together through every channel imaginable. Then he dropped down on one knee and popped the question." She bit her lip. "And I said yes."

"That's awesome!" Mara leapt to her feet and crushed them both into a hug. All of them were laughing. "I'm thrilled for you guys. When's the big day?"

"We're thinking a year out," said Danielle.

"Milk the engagement for all it's worth, right?" said James.

"Hah," said Mara. "That's the spirit." She raised her eyebrows. "You realize, I'm going to be a permanent third wheel right? Best friends and all that."

Danielle and James both laughed and raised their flutes. "That's why we're telling you first, our families don't even know yet," said James.

Mara couldn't keep herself from smiling for the rest of the evening. Conspiracies had plagued Mozaik since its inception but it was also opening so many new doors they could have never imagined on day one.

10

"'DON'T WORK WITH ASSHOLES?'" Sue's face was flushed under her bushy brown curls. "I'm tempted to follow your advice and quit right now." She threw her hands in the air.

Mara did her best to maintain a straight face. "Actually, we're trying to get rid of you. That little piece of advice was a personal tip."

"Phooey," said Sue, narrowing her eyes. "As if I'd believe that for an instant. Do you have any idea how many reporters I'm juggling right now with this whole STEM Education Act thing? Half of them are trying to eviscerate Congress and frame us as a special interest group, the other half think we're some financial messiah. You wouldn't fire me in your wildest dreams. Who else is going to field these wonks? Certainly not you!"

"Sue," said Mara. "If we could bottle your energy, we'd put Red Bull out of business in a heartbeat."

"Energy drinks are for losers who can't generate their own momentum."

"See?" said Mara. "If we recorded your one-liners, you could compete with Confucius for fortune cookie advice."

"Want me to predict your future?" Sue bugged her eyes wide and wiggled her fingers. "Headstrong CEO causes scandal after scandal by not sticking to the notes that her PR advisor carefully prepared. Company goes down in flames."

Mara laughed. "That's why you're our PR guru. To grab the fire extinguisher and make sure Mozaik survives my brusque but charming public image."

"Brusque but charming?" said Sue, incredulous. "Mara, girlfriend, our clients are banks. *Banks!*" She smacked her fist into her opposing palm. "You know what kind of vendors banks like? Boring, reliable, loyal ones. Boring, reliable, and loyal. Not 'brusque but charming.' They don't want to hear about how OCD you get over parking tickets or what your favorite breakfast cereal is. They just want to know we can deliver the goods."

"Speaking of delivering the goods, I've got to get back to work." Mara patted Sue on the shoulder. "Don't worry, I'll do my best to practice being boring."

Sue shook her head in defeat, curls bobbing along.

Mara turned and made her way toward the Fortress of Solitude conference room. Every floor of Mozaik's building had a large open working space surrounded by a ring of private offices and shared conference rooms. Expansive rectangular tables made it look like a techie medieval feast hall. Heavy-duty outlets for power and wired internet snaked down from the ceiling at regular intervals above each table and clusters of people were working on a wide variety of projects. A large Mozaik logo hung from the ceiling in the center of the room above a foosball table. The easel next to it displayed a complex tiered score sheet. A diverse selection of superhero posters dominated any wall that didn't have a window.

Pride rose in Mara's chest. It was hard to believe that this was all real. *Welcome to the hole.* That's what David had said on their hike when Mozaik had yet to land a lead investor for their seed round. Mara had been desperate, sure she would have to get a job at Starbucks or limp back to her parents for support. Now, their team filled an entire building and she was hiring many of her former classmates.

They would need to hire far more and begin looking into companies to put on the acquisition hit list. Vernon had been overrun with customer inquiries in the last ten days. News of the rider in the American STEM Education Act was starting to percolate through the banks and Juliana had referred Mozaik as the benchmark software for compliance. The office had gone from frenzied to frantic as they pulled out all the plugs to keep up with demand.

That's why the board meeting had to go well this afternoon. She needed David and Lars to sign off on their plan to take Mozaik public. It was time to go over her slides one more time.

She opened the door to the Fortress of Solitude and looked back over her shoulder at the hive of activity. These were the people that were going to change the world of finance. They might not know it yet, but the fruits of their labors were going to shape the future of banking. She smiled and slipped into the conference room, shutting the door behind her.

"Hello, Mara," said a quiet voice.

Mara jumped and her hand darted automatically to the holster at the small of her back. Her heart rate skyrocketed and adrenaline surged through her body. She spun to face the room, pistol extended in both hands.

"Is that how you greet your esteemed board members?" Lars raised a single eyebrow. He sat at the far end of the table, dressed in an impeccably tailored charcoal suit. Legs comfortably crossed, he didn't appear at all phased by the loaded handgun pointed at his chest.

For a single disturbing moment, Mara considered pulling the trigger. How poetically that might close this circle jerk of violence and manipulation. The force of the bullet would force the chair to roll back from the table. His blood would splatter all over the whiteboard behind him, dripping down over the bas-relief of stylized shards of ice that lined the walls. It would ruin his perfect suit and wipe the barely concealed smirk from his face. Craig would appreciate the irony of his killer bleeding out in the Fortress of Solitude.

Hands shaking, she slowly lowered the gun. It felt like it weighed a thousand pounds. She flicked the safety back on and returned it to the holster. Cold sweat beaded from every pore. Quinn would tell her to stop being such an amateur. Build a case. Take him down the right way.

"The board meeting doesn't start for another hour," she said, meeting his gaze and trying to keep her shivering under control.

"Ah, well," said Lars. He uncrossed his legs, placed his elbows on the table, and leaned forward. "I'm just ever so excited to check in with my most promising portfolio company. Rumor has it you're doing very, very well."

11

"SO, WHAT DO YOU WANT?" asked Mara. She lowered herself into a chair and tried to slow her breathing. Lars had obviously intended to throw her off balance by showing up early. She needed to calm down, to think rationally. She had overreacted, pulling the gun. That had shown him weakness, not strength. If he could incite this kind of a reaction simply by arriving early to a meeting then he clearly had her on a tight emotional leash.

"Just what any director wants," said Lars. "The best for his company. We're all here to maximize shareholder value."

Mara pulled a notepad and a pen from the stack in the middle of the table, right next to the engraved Superman logo. Across the top she scribbled the date and time, anything to give her a bit of mental breathing room so that she could catch up to this conversation.

"I'm happy to hear it," she said. Her voice was flat, too devoid of tone to be natural. But that was better than the high-pitched squeak that she worried might have come out instead. "That's why we hold board meetings after all. You received the materials two days ago. I'll be giving the update once David arrives at one. After that, I'll be happy to field any questions."

She flashed back to how Dominic's face had gone scarlet when Mara had turned the tables on their initial bid to transform Mozaik's Series A financing into a distressed deal. Lars's face had remained still, like one of the rocks in Boulder Creek. It looked identical now, empty as the mind of a meditating monk.

"I thought we might have a more intimate strategy session before then," said Lars, tapping an index finger on the table. "I've always found that brainstorming is far more effective when the group is small. We can really dig in. I'm only in Boulder every so often, so this is an opportunity not to be missed. Am I right?" His pale gray eyes made it clear that the question was rhetorical.

Despite herself, Mara's mind kept looping like a broken record back to Quinn's death. He had charged from behind the corner of the warehouse, gun blazing. Dominic's head had popped like a crushed melon, pulp flying everywhere. Quinn had been firing her gun. If only she could have stopped him, somehow prevented his suicidal assault. But it had been too late and she had fled the scene with the taste of tears and dust on her tongue.

She bit the inside of her cheek hard. The pain focused her thinking. The hard tang of iron brought her back to the present. She nodded, steeling herself.

"I'm always happy to get shareholder input," she said. "What do you have in mind?"

"Good, good," said Lars. He reached down and fiddled with an attaché case. Then he removed a thick manila envelope and placed it on the table in front of him but made no move to offer it to Mara.

Her heart leapt again. It was exactly the same kind of envelope that had carried Lars's surveillance photos threatening her and James's families.

"What is your plan?" he asked.

Mara bit her cheek again. She couldn't let him get to her like this. It was maddening. She needed to keep it together, stay centered.

"Plan for what?" she asked.

"Why, I thought that would be obvious," he said. "The American STEM Education Act is a coup for Mozaik, a beautiful piece of legislation if I say so myself. Lawmakers are usually so stodgy when it comes to innovation but once in a while, they come through. You must be overwhelmed with new client inquiries."

"We are," said Mara. "We're doing our best to just ensure each gets a considered response at the moment."

"And I assume that means you'll need to grow the business quite dramatically in order to service those new customers?"

"Yes, of course," she said, shaking her head. She had lost her balance and she wasn't going to regain it by letting him control the rhythm of the conversation. "Look, Lars, you've read the update. I will be going over these exact same questions in about forty-five minutes. Why are you here? What do you really want to talk about?"

He cocked his head to one side. "How are you planning to pay for that growth? You'll need to roll up at least a few other companies. I've been over your financials. You certainly don't have the margins or cash to finance it yourselves. You won't be able to get close to enough commercial debt. What will it be? Flirting with private equity for a massive growth round?"

So this was it. James was right. Lars was worried about their growth plan. He didn't want to risk them going public because it would attract oversight and threaten his little game. He had shown up here early just to intimidate her, to show her who was alpha. He wanted to scare them away from doing an IPO. And he had brought along another set of photos to demonstrate his leverage and make his threat explicit.

No sense in beating around the bush. She looked him straight in the eye. "We're going to take Mozaik public. We'll be able to access all the cash we need through the public market and it will establish the company as the leader in the space. We'll use that money to make a number of strategic acquisitions. We'll buy service firms that already work with the banks in order to grow the team quickly and accelerate our go to market."

Lars pressed his lips into a tight smile. "That's exactly what I was hoping you would say."

He slid the manila folder the length of the table. It came to a smooth stop next to her notepad. It was impossible to read his level of irony. She hesitated, then reached down to open it.

"Going public is no small task," said Lars. "You'll need to make some changes around here. You'll need an in-house general counsel, a team of investment bankers, and a CFO who's been through IPOs before. I've already selected the relevant experts for you and you'll find them indispensable. Their background information and résumés are in there." He gestured at the folder. "But don't worry, I've already made very sure they are on board to join the team and guarantee a successful IPO."

Mara didn't know whether to be happy Lars wasn't opposing their plan or frustrated because they had obviously failed to predict his response. She definitely hadn't anticipated this. The cold sweat redoubled.

"Who says board members can't be helpful?" said Lars. "I should have gotten into this whole venture capital game far earlier. It's amazing the impact technology can have." He knitted his fingers together on the conference table. "I really do enjoy working with you, Mara." Her stomach twisted. "I have to admit, you continue to surprise me. Together, the world is our oyster."

He stood and brushed off the front of his suit jacket, favoring the leg that Quinn had injured. "One piece of advice though, don't draw a weapon if you don't plan to use it."

12

THE IMPACT OF HER FEET hitting the pavement reverberated up through Mara's body. One leg shot out in front of the other, rocketing her along the sidewalk. Late afternoon sun had baked all the humidity out of the air.

In her peripheral vision, she saw Xavier half a step behind, letting her set the pace. Going running together was a great cover for a clandestine meeting in Colorado. Nothing blended into the Boulder landscape better than a couple of enthusiastic joggers.

The red stone buildings of CU Boulder's campus paraded by on either side. Maples shaded bright green lawns and the maze of paved paths that brimmed with students embarking on a new academic year. She and James had once been among them. She remembered the confusion of enrolling in her first classes, moving into the dorms, and adjusting to Boulder. Professor Swarson's governance class had been the bane of her existence and nothing could have been more stressful than preparing for the LSATs. It seemed like a lifetime ago.

Her thighs burned and she tried to flush the feeling out on the next exhale. At least she was running more frequently this year. She finally realized that you couldn't wait until you had enough time for exercise. You had to make time for it no matter what. After Lars had ambushed her in the Fortress of Solitude, the actual board meeting had gone as well as could be expected. Of course, that didn't mean much because David and Lars didn't see eye-to-eye on almost anything. Coming out of that meeting, she had a to-do list a mile long. But here she was, going on a run.

They were reaching the edge of campus and she took a left. The rich afternoon light deepened the colors and textures around them. Everything popped, as if seen through a camera filter.

Mara flinched as a stab of pain lanced through her stomach. Damn, that was a bad cramp. She pushed through trying to keep her breath under control, stop it from becoming ragged. But the cramp cinched tighter with every step, twisting a knot in her belly.

She held up a hand and stopped. Bending over she gasped for breath and put her hands on her knees.

"Cramp," she said, sucking at the dry air. "Bad one."

"No problem," said Xavier, coming to a stop next to her. "Hey, isn't this the exact spot where we first met?"

"Huh?" Mara looked up at him. He had on a baby blue quick dry shirt and bright green running shorts that could only be described as dorky. Scuffed New Balance sneakers completed the jogger image. The gray eyes under the short-cropped blonde hair hinted that there was more to the story. She couldn't believe he had recovered from the leg wound so quickly. His gait gave no indication of the injury, despite the ghastly scarring.

"This is where you ran into me and knocked my coffee over," he said.

She looked around, panting. He was right. *Don't worry about it. It was Starbucks piss anyway. Their roast isn't worth the cups it's poured into.* She had been crying, running from Craig's betrayal. He had parked his Jeep right there at the curb. She could still remember the excitement on his face as he revealed his big surprise, that he had been secretly investigating the Center for Mathematics and Society. She could see the brick building now, beyond a line of trees. How quickly that excitement had collapsed when she broke up with him and dashed away from the car. But Craig was beyond all excitement or despondency now. He was dead. Murdered along with Derrick and Quinn to protect Maelstrom.

Weren't cramps supposed to recede when you took a breather? This one seemed intent on tearing her insides apart.

"Remind me," she said, between shuddering breaths. "Why we can't nail his ass to a fucking wall right now."

Xavier glanced around quickly. "Mara, I don't think this—"

She waved the comment away. "We don't have phones here. Nobody's recording us."

"We've talked about this," he said, voice low. "Investigations take time. Years. We've acquired more intelligence on Maelstrom in the past fourteen months than in the preceding decade. We want the case against them to be airtight. When we strike, it needs to be a fatal blow."

"I almost shot him yesterday," she said. It seemed almost funny now.

"What?" Xavier was serious now, despite her light tone. "Mara, what the hell are you talking about?" He put his hands on her shoulders, looking directly into her eyes.

She shook him off. "Don't worry, I didn't actually shoot him. I *almost* did." She spat on the ground next to them. "He snuck into one of our conference rooms and ambushed me before the board meeting. It scared the living shit out of me. I pulled the gun before I even saw who he was. Once I realized it was Lars, well, that made me want to actually use the gun."

"Mara." He paused, as if unsure what to say next. Mara glanced away as a group of laughing students passed them.

"Mara," he said again, moving his face to intercept her line of vision. "Look, you could have pulled that trigger. You could have killed him. But then where would we be? Do you think your family, friends, and employees would be happy seeing you convicted of murder? Is that what Craig would have wanted? Or Quinn? I can only imagine how terrible you must feel having to interact with him. But we have to play the long game here."

"And while we're playing the long game, how many lives will they destroy?" Bile rose into Mara's mouth. "Who gets to make that cost-benefit decision?"

He grimaced. "If all we do is take down Lars, how long do you think it will take for someone else to take his place? There are already probably half a dozen lieutenants in Maelstrom waiting in the wings to do just that. If we play our hand too early, we flush away years of work and risk."

She pressed her hand against her abdomen, trying to massage out the cramp. "We're going to take Mozaik public," she said.

"What?" he said, taken aback.

"We've already started preparing the S1," she said.

"That's... amazing," said Xavier. He rubbed his sweaty chin. "How long will the process take?"

"Apparently about six months," she said. Pressing deeper to get at the cramp. "Assuming everything goes to plan."

"And then you'll be ringing a bell on Wall Street?"

"What do you think? Should I wear this?" She gestured down at her tattered CU Boulder t-shirt and form-fitting yoga pants.

"Hah, that would certainly make an impression."

"Can you tell me something?" She gave up on the cramp and stood up straight. "Why would Lars want us to go public?"

"What do you mean? Aren't investors generally thrilled at the prospect of an IPO? He'll be able to sell some of his shares for a pretty penny." Xavier frowned. "But you know that better than I do."

"Right," she said. "But Lars isn't just any investor. He's got a lot to hide. We had assumed that we'd have to battle him to approve the decision to take Mozaik public. There's no way he wants that kind of oversight. It'll make it harder for him to directly manipulate us. We'll have audited quarterly financial reporting. If anything looks funny, the SEC will be up our asses faster than a street racer on meth."

"Nice mental image," he said.

"Seriously, though," said Mara. "What do you think he's playing at?"

Xavier kneaded his thigh as he stared off into space. It was the first time on this run that Mara had seen him do anything to indicate that the injury might still bother him.

"I don't know anything about IPOs," he said. His gaze refocused on her. "But if I'm trying to figure out motive, I always start by identifying who has the most to gain."

"You think that he just wants to cash out his shares?"

"I doubt he'll mind a nice cash infusion but Lars doesn't strike me as the kind of guy to favor quick flips," said Xavier. "He's probably already earned more, because you guys blew up his chief rivals within Maelstrom last year, than he'll make on your IPO. No, my guess is that this is part of some larger play. Mozaik going public must benefit him in some other way."

Mara sighed. "And what might that be?" she asked.

He shook his head. "Your guess is as good as mine. We'll add it to our list though. If I come across anything useful, I'll let you know."

"Aren't spies supposed to know these kinds of things? Isn't that the whole point of a having a Special Task Force on Cyber Finance?"

"Spies like me," he said, "are supposed to get people like you to help us figure out what's really going on."

"And my tax money is paying your salary." It was a joke, not a jab. "No wonder the country is such a mess."

He smiled wide. "Although human intelligence may sometimes sound like an oxymoron, it's still often the only way to know what's really going on."

UNCOMMON STOCK | 47

"Let's get on with this workout," she said, frowning.

"Lead the way."

She started out along the walkway, picking up the pace. Out of the corner of her eye, she caught glimpses of the Center through the line of trees. It quickly disappeared from view but loitered in the shadows of her thoughts.

13

MARA'S PALMS WERE as wet as a Portland winter. Her thumbs drummed on the steering wheel. She had parked down the block from the cul-de-sac. She ran her tongue along the inside of her teeth.

She should have reached out and offered support immediately. But she hadn't. Not for Craig. Not for Quinn. Her breath was high in her chest.

Reaching over, she grabbed the bouquet of flowers on the passenger seat and then stepped out of the car. The idyllic sheen of the suburban Denver neighborhood grated against the emotional turmoil in her gut. Had Quinn taught Craig to ride a bike around this cul-de-sac? Did he argue about mowing the lawn and the rest of his chores while he was growing up?

Violent death didn't have a place in neighborhoods like this. The sun beat down on manicured gardens and the sky was a blank blue, not a cloud in sight. Sure, a grandmother might pass away, but that was to be expected. Everyone gets there one day. The circle of life and all that. But a father following in the footsteps of his murdered son?

This wasn't a favela in Rio or a project in Baltimore. Kids from here got good grades. They went to college. Maybe they betrayed the hopes of their middle class parents by dropping out of med school to move back into the basement to start working on a novel. Some probably struggled with drugs and addiction. You never knew what might go on behind the tasteful curtains. But you did know that it didn't involve two family members being gunned down because of a criminal conspiracy they were in the process of investigating.

The brown paper wrapped around the bouquet crinkled and Mara relaxed her grip on the flowers. Pasadena was another place where these things weren't supposed to happen. But the Taiwanese mafia had proven that truism wrong when they assassinated James's uncle at a family picnic. Nightmares of that day fermented in her subconscious and left her tangled in sheets soaked with cold sweat.

The house sat there like nothing was amiss. The first time she had been here, she had arrived with a six-pack, not a bouquet. If only there was a way to turn back the clock. She could stop Quinn from rushing out to confront Dominic and Lars. She could call off Craig's amateur investigation of the Center. She could stop James from hacking the Center in the first place. Years later, they could all laugh it off over a beer.

Instead, here she was. Delivering flowers and empty words to the sole surviving resident of a house in the sad corner of a planned development. The path connecting the sidewalk to the front door was paved with brick. She squared her shoulders, pushed down the lump in her throat, and marched toward the door.

She stopped at the threshold. The door stared back at her, blank and turquoise and imposing. She raised a hand to ring the bell. Maria had been a shell at Quinn's funeral. Lost on the shoals of disbelief. Craig's death had shredded their marriage, eating away at the seams before unraveling the entire thing. But losing an estranged husband so soon after a son was unthinkable.

Mara remembered Maria's eyes from the funeral. Before, they had been bright, knowing, sly. Now, they were windows into a soul hollowed out by grief. Nothing was left but a husk. A watermelon reduced to rind by countless insatiable mouths.

What could Mara have said? What could she say now? Craig and Quinn would be alive today if it wasn't for her. *Sorry, I killed your son and your husband? Is there anything I can do to help even though it won't change anything?* A bereft mother and wife didn't need solace from such as Mara. She would be nothing but a rude intrusion, a reminder of pain that was still all too fresh. Wounds like that don't heal. They fester.

Her finger wavered. She lowered it, bell un-rung. Stooping, she laid the flowers on the doorstep as she had so many times before. And then she was running back along the bricks, along the sidewalk past all the well-kept houses, until she collapsed, sobbing, into the driver's seat. Somewhere on the freeway back to Boulder, the tears dried up.

14

"THIS ISN'T HOW IT'S SUPPOSED TO GO," said Vernon. He threw the manila envelope onto Mara's desk. Some of the papers inside scattered out of it as the file landed. James sat next to him.

"We need investment bankers to run the IPO," said Mara.

"Normally we'd interview a bunch of them and then select three or four to sell our IPO," said Vernon. "Lars has already pre-negotiated favorable terms with them and handed us the team fully baked. They've already established the deal economics as well."

James swiped the hair out of his face. "But isn't that a good thing?"

Vernon shook his head. "It's not right. It's not his place as a board member to do any of this. We're the management team. We're the ones saddled with riding Mozaik through the IPO rodeo. If we don't choose our bankers and we don't set the terms, how much leverage will we have actually working with them?"

"At least they're external," said James.

"They're not all external," said Mara. "The lawyer and new CFO will be in-house."

"Sure," said Vernon. "But even the external bankers will have a massive influence on the success of this company. The IPO depends on us collaborating closely with them. One fuckup could have dramatic, lasting impacts on Mozaik. This short circuits the whole process."

"Do you really think we'd get more favorable economics elsewhere?" asked Mara. "They're committed to raising $200 million on a $1.1 billion valuation. Are you saying we could do better?"

Vernon frowned. "Those are great numbers," he said. "But the proof is in the pudding. I'm not saying we could do better, I'm saying that it's not really our deal. Lars laid out the whole thing. It makes me extremely uncomfortable. They've got to actually be able to sell that to the market. Nothing would be worse than going out strong and beating down value once we see The Book."

James raised his hands. "Vernon, you said this would short circuit the whole process." Vernon nodded. "If the terms of the deal are good and the people in question have strong track records, then doesn't that mean we're closer to IPO than we would be otherwise?"

They sat in silence for a moment. Mara leaned back in her chair and crossed her arms.

"Well, Vernon?" she asked.

"James is right," said Vernon, clenching a fist. "On paper, this is great. It eliminates months of work for us." He pursed his lips. "But it makes me uncomfortable. If we didn't select the team, who are they really working for?"

"Okay," said Mara. "I share your concern. It's obviously odd for Lars to have put this together for us. But, for now, I can't see a problem with playing along. If we push back and reject the team, we'd have to start assembling a replacement from square one anyway."

"If we push back," said James, looking down. "I think we will have much bigger issues to worry about." Powerlessness infected his tone.

The temperature in the room seemed to drop. Mara became conscious of the holster at her back. Vernon shrugged and his expression turned glum.

"Alright," said Mara, her voice quiet. "We may not know Lars's endgame, but we certainly want Mozaik's public offering to succeed." She stacked the papers scattered around her desk and slid them back into the manila envelope. "For the moment, we'll proceed with his team. I'm going to go talk to Gordon."

15

MARA FOUND GORDON IN HIS OFFICE. Disco music played softly from his computer. He was pecking keys with his right hand and squeezing a bright green stress ball in his left. Ironic motivational posters plastered the walls. *Believe in yourself, because the rest of us think you're an idiot. Economics, the science of explaining tomorrow why the predictions you made yesterday didn't come true today. Taxes, you can't always get what you want, but if you try sometimes, you just might find you can get what you need taken from you by the government.*

A smile stole across Mara's lips. Gordon was an oddball, no doubt about it. But she had to admit he had grown on her since he had joined the team. Because Dominic had referred him, they had long suspected he might be ferreting intel on Mozaik back to Maelstrom. That had strained their already awkward relationship. But that theory had proved to be a red herring and he had earned a reputation as a competent CFO, even if he was a curmudgeon.

She steeled herself and knocked on the inside of his doorframe. He turned from the screen, the chair creaking under his bulk.

"Ahh," he said. "The woman of the hour."

She stepped forward and sat down across from him. "Gordon, I think you know why I'm here."

"Time for the guillotine then," he said, smiling sadly. He muted the music, looked around. "Well, I have enjoyed my time here, despite appearances. Now I can add a tech startup notch to my belt. I've never had to approve spend on interior design for superhero conference rooms before. Don't worry, I won't cause trouble. Just let me pack up my stuff."

"What?" Mara held up her hands, appalled. "No. Gordon, we're not firing you."

He had already opened a drawer, presumably to empty it. "But I've never been through an IPO before," he said. "I'm not the right guy for you, for Mozaik. You'll need someone who knows that process back to front."

She nodded. "You're right. We have a new CFO arriving tomorrow along with a lawyer and a team of bankers. But if you're willing to continue here, we'd prefer not to lose you. You know our financials better than anyone and the new CFO will need to get oriented before he'll be able to polish our numbers up to public reporting standards."

She gestured toward the drawer. "I understand if you don't want to take a demotion and are ready to move on. But we would love to have you head our accounting department moving forward."

He looked at her. "You're serious?"

She nodded. "I wouldn't joke about something like this."

Out of nowhere, she saw a tear course down his cheek and over his chins. He rubbed it away with the back of his hand. "I'm sorry," he said. "I didn't mean to..."

For a moment she wasn't sure how to react, then she moved around the desk and put an arm around his shoulder. "It's okay," she said. "Really, it's okay."

"I just—" He sniffled. "Dominic got me every job I've ever had," he said. "We've known each other since high school. With him gone," he shrugged, "I just didn't know what I was going to do next."

Mara suppressed a shiver, remembering Dominic's violent death. The taste of gravel, dust, and desperation filled her mouth.

She shook her head, trying to clear it. Even manipulative assholes must have friends.

"We need you here," she said, patting Gordon on the back. "Now more than ever."

She looked up at the wall and shivered. *Ambition, the journey of a thousand miles sometimes ends very, very badly.* She could only hope that they were on a better path.

16

_____

MARA STEPPED THROUGH the swinging doors, leaving the warm summer evening behind. Taj was richly appointed. White tablecloths covered circular tables of different sizes that were scattered around the room like polka dots. Large-format canvas prints of Indian countryside juxtaposed the brilliant green of rice paddies with the ruddy exposed brick walls. Mid-century ceiling fans spun lazily, wafting the rich smells from the open kitchen that took up the back of the space. A huge photo of the Taj Mahal hung from the ceiling toward the rear, delineating the boundary between the kitchen and the seating area.

She spotted David at a table along the wall and weaved through the other diners to join him. Eschewing his usual wool sweater, David had on a Hawaiian shirt alive with colorful psychedelic designs. His hair exploded from his scalp in an unruly halo of frizz. He smiled as she sat across from him.

"Long time, no see," he said.

"Yeah, yeah," she said. "We seem to be making a habit of these post-board meeting dinners."

He pushed his glasses up the bridge of his nose. She marveled at how much he looked like a crazy professor. He was a veteran serial entrepreneur who most people would probably guess was teaching theoretical physics at CU. In other words, the polar opposite of the new team members who had arrived today at Lars's behest.

"Most companies hold board dinners," said David. "But it's been two weeks since the board meeting and normally the entire Board attends."

"Well, right now we have two thirds of Mozaik's board at this table," she said. "And I get the feeling that you'd prefer we leave that last third out of it anyway."

David nodded. "I won't pretend to be a friend of Lars."

"And I wouldn't want you to," she said.

He held up a menu. "Priorities," he said.

The food was served family style. They started with papadums served with pickled peppers, green beans, cucumbers and fresh mint and apple chutney. There was also blood orange salad with chicories and pistachios as well as Brussels sprouts sautéed in chaat masala. A bottle of Pinot Gris sweated in an ice bucket on the table.

"So," said David, "you're taking Mozaik public."

"It certainly appears that way," said Mara, grinning. "We're filing the Confidential S-1 next week."

"I've got to say," said David. "I've never had a company do a drag race IPO based on a guaranteed regulatory monopoly. We're in virgin territory here."

"Well, I'm popping my Wall Street cherry too, so we're even," she said.

"Fair enough," he said.

"I've never seen so many suits at Mozaik before," she said. "Our new CFO, GC, and bankers arrived last week. They're certainly industrious. The CFO and GC are camped out in a conference room pulling all the pieces together. Essentially they helicopter into the lives of our different department heads and find new ways to piss them off."

David snorted and dipped a papadum in chutney. "Going public requires that you operate like a public company. That means a lot more standardization and financial controls than you're used to. I took Ooba public in '99 and that was enough for me. I kept my next two companies private until they were acquired. Didn't want to deal with the paperwork."

"It's a grind, but it'll give us the resources we need to go global," she said. "Vernon is already discreetly opening some doors at potential acquisition targets. Larsons, AMQ, and Udemas are at the top of his hit list."

"I have to hand it to you, Mara," he said. "You've accomplished an enormous amount in such a short period of time. It's a testament to your leadership, you've made amazing strides over the past year. Remember when we were talking about your equity split with James? Or how he hacked The Center? That wasn't long ago." His eyes sparkled behind the glasses. "Now, you're going public and your code is going to be running at every bank on the planet, or close enough."

"It's been a team effort that would have been impossible without helping hands of friends like you and Juliana." She paused, letting the diverse spices dance and sparkle on her tongue. "But sometimes I'm not so sure we've come very far at all. I thought it was going to get easier, but we're just dealing with bigger and bigger problems."

"If you think it's going to get easier, you definitely shouldn't go public," said David.

"What do you mean by that?"

"Most entrepreneurs think that an IPO is their big ticket to riches," he said. "If you successfully raise on the valuation we discussed in the board meeting, you and James will each instantly have hundreds of millions of dollars on paper. But it's only on paper." He sipped his wine, colors reflecting off of the condensation on the glass. "Going public is a new beginning, not an exit. You can't sell your shares during the IPO or even soon thereafter. You're signing on to build the business for the long-term, with all the ugliness, frustration, and success that could ultimately bring you."

He raised an eyebrow. "If you're looking for a big cash payout," he said. "Acquisition can be better for founders. If someone buys you out, you can walk away rich. This is different. I'll be able to sell my preferred shares during the IPO if I want to, Maelstrom will too. But you and your team will keep your stakes or risk tanking your own stock. Nobody wants to see a management team dumping shares on the open market."

"Because we would be demonstrating a lack of confidence in our own company."

"Exactly."

"We're not in this for the money," said Mara. A big paycheck certainly wouldn't hurt though. "We want to make a real impact. We want to clean up a dirty business. You know that." She sipped her wine. "What do I need to know about the IPO process?"

"That's a big question."

"That's why I've got advisers like you."

"Hah. Well, it's like launching a space shuttle, lots of tedious preparation followed by a short period of extreme stress. Your new lawyer will walk you through the minutiae. But there are two things you should keep in mind."

He ripped off a steaming piece of fresh naan and scooped up some chicken. "I almost fainted during Ooba's road show. We were doing half a dozen pitches a day, usually in different cities. One day we had breakfast in Hollywood and lunch in Austin. I was so worked up talking to the investors in L.A. that I forgot to eat. We spent the flight prepping for Austin and the group we talked to there had so many questions that I didn't have time for lunch. Then we flew to Chicago. I got dizzy and almost fell as we disembarked. I had to sit down for a few minutes before we could take a cab to the hotel. I realized it was late afternoon and all I had consumed the whole day were three cups of bad coffee. So make sure to sit down every chance you get, and when there's food, eat."

"Sage advice. Luckily, I'm pretty good at the eating part." She smiled and raised a fork loaded with Brussels sprouts.

"Oh," said David. "And my other piece of wisdom? Don't fuck it up. IPOs go sideways all the time. There are so many balls in the air that it's all too easy for one to get dropped. Even if everyone pulls their weight, something totally beyond your control can mess it up. One of my portfolio companies was planning to go public in 2011. They had their S1 in hand and the road show went extremely well. But two days before they rang the bell, a patent troll from Seattle dropped a nuisance lawsuit on them and that evening their lead banker missed a meeting. Turned out he had died of a cocaine overdose. They had to delay the listing and the price floor fell out from under them. In the end, they withdrew altogether and wrote off the whole exercise as an expensive diversion."

"You're really trying to get me excited about this, aren't you?" She grinned.

He smiled grimly. "Going public is going to change Mozaik from the ground up. Hope for the best, plan for the worst."

Her expression sobered. Things were already changing inside the company. The faces matching the names in Lars's manila envelope had arrived last week. Leslie Yee was Mozaik's new GC, their internal lawyer. Grant Hughes, the new CFO, looked like someone had taken him straight out of a mixed martial art ring and stuffed him into a suit. Zach Hildegard was their immaculate lead banker, every inch of his appearance tailored as carefully as his track record of public filings.

Grant had taken over Gordon's role as CFO and was restructuring their financial reporting. Leslie was using her prerogative as general counsel to usher in new bureaucratic management processes into every department. Zach and his bankers called it the "tune up" phase. There was an endless checklist of compliance items they needed to address in order to ensure their S1 passed muster with the SEC, and that Mozaik could weather an audit. It was a lot of legwork, none of which was improving their product or directly serving their customers. Needless to say, the changes weren't popular among the Mozaik rank and file.

On the other hand, everyone on the team was excited that the company was going public. Of course, there was the fact that the IPO would fund the massive hiring and acquisition spree needed to service their worldwide customer base. But there was more to it than operational requirements or strategic angles of attack. It was a huge vote of confidence for a company that was less than two years old. Seeing stock options skyrocket in value didn't hurt either.

"Now," David leaned forward. The sparkle in his eyes distilled into laser focus. "How long have you known this was coming?"

"What do you mean?" The sharpness in his tone had thrown her off balance.

"Come on, Mara," said David. "I wasn't born yesterday. Deciding on whether or not to pursue an IPO takes months of weighing different options. Identifying, vetting, and selecting the right bankers can often take many more months of negotiation on terms and deal economics. Engineering regulatory capture like Juliana's rider requires long-term lobbying effort. We haven't heard about any of these things at previous board meetings. Then this week you walk in with an entire roadmap for an IPO including team and terms."

"We didn't lobby Juliana." This conversation was skittering far too close to the shadows. "She pushed that bill through and only told us about it after it passed. She explained it to me in the Rose Garden two weeks ago. She was just impressed by what we accomplished together with DVG."

David sipped his wine. "Okay. If you didn't know about the bill until two weeks ago, then how the hell did you start the IPO process moving so quickly? It just doesn't make sense."

Mara wiped her mouth with her napkin and tried to collect her thoughts. David knew that Maelstrom had tried to manipulate Mozaik's first financing to achieve draconian terms. But he didn't know that Lars was responsible for murder or that he had leverage over her and James that went far beyond an unfair contract. Anyone who knew what Lars was really up to was necessarily endangered by that knowledge. They had only shared the secret with those who absolutely needed to know. The only members of that inner circle were James, Vernon, Xavier, and herself.

The chair creaked as David leaned back. Was there a specific, actionable reason for her to tell David? She would love to simply get his advice on the situation, and he wouldn't be able to give useful input without more details. She chewed her lip. That was selfish. She would be putting him in harm's way just to give her the opportunity to pick his brain. That wasn't fair to anyone, least of all him. She had to hold the tiller and contribute what she could to Xavier and CyFi along the way.

Mara sighed. "David, remember when I tried to bullshit you while we were at Ota sushi?"

He nodded without breaking eye contact.

"You stood up and almost left right in the middle of our meal," she said. "Well, I'm not going to do that again, here. Instead, I'm going to do something that you'll probably like even less. I'm not going to tell you what's really going on."

David frowned. The fans whirred above them, against the background hum of conversation. Waiters dodged from table to table, trays loaded with steaming plates of food. An ambient electronic reimagining of Indian folk music piped over the sound system.

"I could sit here and tell you that we just worked our asses off and put that roadmap together." She swallowed. "But we'd both know I wasn't telling the whole truth. I wish I could share what's going on behind the scenes. But I can't and I won't. David, I need you to trust me on this."

17

DANIELLE PASSED BY THE CONFERENCE ROOM WINDOW holding a to-go box, probably on her way back from picking up lunch.

"Alright, time to go through another set of COGS numbers from last year," said Grant.

Mara looked back at the mountain of paperwork spread out on the conference table between them. They were working out of the Batcave and Mara had never spelunked through bureaucratic caverns this deep. Their team needed to cross every t and dot every i before handing their S1 over to the SEC for review. Spreadsheets and legalese had become her raison d'être as she worked with Grant, Zach, and Leslie to assemble the requisite materials.

"Give me five minutes," said Mara. "There's someone I need to talk to and I think we could both use a quick break."

Grant shrugged, muscle-bound shoulders threatening to rip the seams of his suit. He was balding with a fringe of close-cropped brown hair.

"Okay," he said. "But we have to get this done today."

"Five minutes," Mara held up a hand, fingers splayed. "Promise." She ducked down and grabbed the slim cardboard cylinder from where she had stashed it in the corner.

Grant was already immersed in his email inbox as she pushed through the door and into the busy common space beyond.

Mozaik employees were hard at work hacking code, scribbling on whiteboards, and settling debates via foosball. She smiled as she circled the large room. Their team was remaking finance and the IPO would set them on an even more frenetic course.

Mara reached the right office. She knocked and pushed it open. Danielle looked up from her desk. A piece of sushi dangled from a pair of chopsticks and her free hand used a mouse to scroll around the screen in front of her.

Danielle smiled. "Hey Mara, what's up?" Mara had to make a conscious effort not to be unnerved by the intensity of her gaze. It carried the promise of dogged absorption, of looking at life with the same rigor that a radiologist might analyze an x-ray.

"I've got something for you." Mara sat down and held up the cardboard cylinder. She would think of something else for James, but this was just too perfect for Danielle.

Frowning, Danielle balanced the chopsticks in the sushi tray. She looked the cylinder up and down, running her hands along it. Then she popped the plastic cap off one end and peered inside.

Mara laughed. "Just take it out. You won't be able to see it otherwise."

Danielle made a quizzical expression and then shook the rolled up glossy paper out of the protective case. She pinched two opposing corners and unrolled it.

"It's one of the original theatrical posters for Pulp Fiction," said Mara. "None of the traditional engagement gifts felt right. I wanted to find something that you might actually like."

Danielle stared at it. Uma Thurman lay on top of a bed, smoking a cigarette, lips blood red against a face pale as milk. Her legs crossed behind her, high heels in the air. An open book and a handgun rested on the mattress in front of her. The movie title, tagline, and names of the stars were scrawled in garish reds and yellows.

The silence stretched on for a few seconds. For the first time,

Mara doubted the choice of gift. Was this inappropriate? Did Danielle just not like it after all? James had admitted that they had first hooked up after watching Pulp Fiction. Was this embarrassing instead of thoughtful?

"It's as if the whole movie is contained in just one expression," said Danielle. "Her face says it all. Sex. Violence. Intrigue. Disdain. Style." A wry look flashed across Danielle's face, the fault line revealing a deeply buried urbanity. "You know what my mom sent me when I told her we got engaged? A set of silverware. *Silverware!* I mean, seriously? I've always been a mystery to my parents. They're sweet but they just don't get it." She turned to Mara, solemn again. "Thank you for this. It's not completely lame."

Mara reached across the desk and drew her into a hug. Danielle resisted at first but then gave in. She and James were a good match. Only someone with Danielle's potency could redirect his sometimes-debilitating single-mindedness. Only someone with his goofiness could get her to take herself less seriously.

They withdrew and Danielle's face flushed. It was funny to think that James was engaged. Not so long ago, Mara had been the one experienced with romantic relationships. She had shared tips and war stories. Now he was living with his fiancé, and she had nothing to show for it but a secret agent fuck buddy. She didn't want to be with James. But she envied what he and Danielle shared.

"I'm truly happy for you guys," said Mara, pushing down the unexpected rush of jealousy. "It's good to see the Mozaik family become a reality."

"I appreciate it, Mara," said Danielle, "Thanks again."

"Alright," said Mara. "Now I've got to sign off on some spreadsheets before Grant has a seizure. Apparently, the SEC waits for no one."

18

A BEAD OF SWEAT dribbled in Mara's eye. She tried to blink it away to no avail. If only she could wipe it away with the back of her hands. But her hands were spread wide against the climbing wall, fingertips barely hanging on to crimpy holds.

She wished she had a firmer grip on Mozaik. Ever since Juliana's revelation, things had been moving too fast to keep track of. *A drag race IPO.* David had been right about that.

She resigned herself to endure the burning sensation and looked up for the next hold. It was a bright purple sloper, a smooth bulbous protrusion that would afford only minimal traction. Twisting her body up and to the right, she stretched her left hand up and slapped it onto the hold. She spread her palm wide to maximize surface area and gripped it like a basketball. Then she shot her right hand up to grab the opposite side.

Leslie, Grant, and Zach had hit the ground running. She had to give them credit for that. Lars had short-circuited the entire preparation and underwriter selection process by assigning them. They had proceeded to arrange the org meeting to kick off the IPO process within a few days and were holding drafting sessions for the Confidential S-1 this weekend. Next week they planned to send it to the SEC for review. The review process would take about three months and then they'd go straight into the road show and take the company public. All in all, they were compressing what would normally take at least a year into four months.

Her cheek rested against the rough composite of the gym's wall. She raised her left foot and smeared the soft rubber of her shoe along the rough surface, creating enough friction to hold part of her weight. Keeping her center of balance as close to the wall as possible, she inched her right foot up and found a notch to slot her toe into.

Was it possible that Lars was helping them because he wanted Mozaik to be successful? Mara had discounted the possibility almost right away but it wasn't outside the realm of possibility. She couldn't even bring him to mind without igniting coals of rage in her gut. But he was a shareholder. Maelstrom would be able to sell their stake in Mozaik for more than a 200x return. Those numbers would make any investor giddy. It was enough to make a reputation from scratch and support an entire portfolio of write-offs. "Home run" would be an understatement.

Pushing off with her legs, she leapt up and grabbed the next hold with both hands. It was shaped like a half-moon and had a deep pocket that she jammed her fingers into. She twisted her leg up and slid her right foot onto the purple sloper that was now at waist level.

Maybe Maelstrom's darker operations were struggling and Lars saw Mozaik's IPO as the fastest way to access badly needed cash. If nine out of ten venture-backed startups failed, what was the hit rate for black market investments? Leslie, Grant, and Zach were putting everything in order for the IPO faster than she and James would ever have been able to organize on their own. Despite the suspicions she harbored with James and Vernon, they had done an exemplary job so far.

She had suspected Gordon of collusion with Maelstrom since the day he set foot in Mozaik. But he had proved to be a competent

CFO and Mara couldn't really imagine the secret agent of a cartel starting to cry because he thought he might have lost his job.

She stood up to reach for the rim of the bouldering wall, a square of bright green tape marking the end of the climb. But as her fingers fought to find purchase along the top of the wall, her foot slid off of the sloper and she fell back away from the wall. She snatched desperately with her fingers but her knee cracked against the hold and she hurtled toward the ground.

Time slowed. Motes of chalk dust hung in the air, beams from the bulbs high on the warehouse ceiling highlighting the constellations of particulates. The gray wall and its peppering of primary color holds receded from view. She should have asked someone to spot her on this climb. Topping out on this route was tough.

The floor smashed into her back, knocking all the air out of her lungs. Stars sparkled in her vision as she gasped. Pain lanced out through her body like she had stuck her finger into an electrical outlet.

"Are you okay?"

She shook her head and tried to blink away the dancing spots. Sucking in another desperate lungful of air, she wiggled her toes and fingers. She was okay. The padded floor prevented her from getting seriously injured.

"I'm fine," she said as soon as she had the enough oxygen. "My foot slipped off that damn sloper."

"Sucks," said one of the climbers leaning over her. "It's a tricky finish. Next time just ask for some beta."

"Yeah," she said, taking the hand he offered and pulling herself up to a sitting position. "Thanks."

They moved off to work on their next bouldering problem. Mara crossed her legs and tried to regulate her breathing. She rotated her torso side-to-side. Her back was going to be tight tomorrow. Her knee throbbed and she pulled her knee close, examining it. A splotch of red showed where it had hit the hold coming down. She gritted her teeth and pushed the pain away.

Perhaps the IPO was Lars's endgame. But he had shown up to the board meeting with all the arrangements already made. That had only been a week after Juliana's revelation. David was right. That was simply too tight of a timeline. Plus, she herself had decided not to share the details with David. Why had she needed to hide anything if this was an above-the-table play? *He's probably already earned more, because you guys blew up his chief rivals within Maelstrom last year, than he'll make on your IPO. No, my guess is that this is part of some larger play. Mozaik going public must benefit him in some other way.* That's what Xavier had said and she couldn't refute the logic.

Mozaik going public could be the payoff Lars was after, but there was no room for assumptions given the stakes of this game. She needed to figure out what his ulterior motive might be.

19

MARA'S KNEE THROBBED like a dubstep bassline. She wrapped a dishtowel around the ice pack, poured two fingers of scotch into a tumbler, and went back to the couch. Sitting back against a cushion, she raised her leg and balanced the ice pack on her knee. A sigh escaped her lips at the sudden coolness.

That had been her first real fall in two years. Usually she could feel something slip and had enough time to recover or at least make a controlled landing. Today she had been taken by surprise. She was getting rusty, not enough time on the rock wall.

She reached over and grabbed her laptop from the coffee table next to the couch. The screen glowed to life and she opened Google. The cursor blinked below the multicolored logo. She ran her fingertips across the keyboard, feeling the smooth surface of the keys.

If Lars had something up his sleeve, how exactly was she supposed to find out what his plans were? She tapped at the touchpad absently. He certainly wouldn't be posting about it on some online forum. She shifted her weight on the cushion.

Lars had given her his manila envelope of instructions and résumés. He had given it to her prior to the board meeting. That meant he had wanted her alone. He didn't want to do it in front of David.

The first sip of whiskey burned like caramel napalm. There were many reasons Lars might not have wanted David to see him giving her directions. It was certainly unusual for any board member to get so involved in the operational minutiae of companies they directed. It would be even more unusual for a CEO to unequivocally acquiesce to such demands. But given Lars's ever-present threat of violent retribution, she had no choice but to capitulate.

She pushed her fingers into her thigh and rubbed, trying to get blood moving around her knee. The funny part was that Lars's instructions were spot on. They established a clear, fast road map to take Mozaik public and included the team she would need to do it successfully. So Lars wasn't avoiding David's oversight because the envelope was incriminating. He had approached her before the board meeting in order to streamline the delivery of his instructions. It allowed her to follow them without David questioning her obedience.

Looking down, she saw her knuckles were white. She unclenched her fists and rebalanced the ice pack. That obedience rankled every part of her. In this case it seemed irrational. Along with the rest of her management team, she had decided to pursue an IPO before Lars had gotten involved. It was the next logical step for Mozaik and the best way to finance the enormous fire hose of demand they were trying to service. Juliana's rider meant they had many more clients than Vernon could book. They could implement the code tomorrow but Mozaik would need to hire hordes more people and buy up entire service companies to provide the support those clients required.

Xavier's job was to investigate criminals like Lars. So far, they had heeded his advice to stay quiet and play the long game. But sometimes the long game felt like the forever game.

In the meantime, acceding to any demand from Lars made her feel dirty. It tainted her excitement for the IPO like hearing the wrong chord in a familiar song.

Turning away from the screen she looked out of the window. Lights glowed in the surrounding buildings. A car parallel parked on the road below. A billboard a few blocks away displayed a smiling toddler frolicking in a field of daisies with a pharmaceutical firm's logo in the corner. Dancing children representing a drug company? Who came up with this stuff?

Her gaze meandered back to the accusing cursor. Lars had played them so deftly during the DVG scandal. She had been convinced that their sting would take him down but he had anticipated her rebelliousness and redirected their efforts to take down his rivals and solidify his power base. She couldn't afford to be so foolish again. He very well might be expecting her to do the opposite of whatever directions he gave. She needed to plan many moves ahead.

But where to start? Lars was good at his job but he was human. It was just as dangerous to overestimate him as to underestimate him. Humans made mistakes. There must be some rock she could turn over, some question they hadn't yet thought to ask.

This hadn't started with the decision to go public. That had become necessary only after Juliana's revelation. The rider. The bill. Her fingers pecked at the keys.

The American STEM Education Act. Section after section of dense congressional prose poured up the screen as she read. Rampant cross-references to various subsections and endless numbered lists made dissecting the language a herculean task. They had all been through the Mozaik-specific subsection many times but she had never tried to digest the entire piece of legislation.

Minutes passed like hours. Reading the bill was slow, deliberate work. The heat of the whiskey helped to counteract the sharp chill of the ice pack. No wonder politicians drank so much of the stuff. They needed something to get them through the legalese. At least that studying for the LSAT was coming in hardy, it made the text more comprehensible.

The glow of the screen was making her eyes feel tired. She let them wander for a moment, relishing the mental break. That damn billboard again. It was front-lit. The girl's dress against the grass was a riot of color in the dark of the surrounding night. A knot tightened in Mara's stomach. She stared at the billboard for a full ten seconds. The icepack slid off her knee, forgotten.

Snapping back to the computer, she cycled back through the browser to the page through which she had accessed the bill. Instead of clicking on the bill to read the text, she opened the voting record.

Holy shit. There it was. Right up at the top. Senator Hartfer stared out at her from the screen. His canned smile sent tremors up her spine. Her thoughts twitched toward the gun that was lying on her bedside table. She could taste bile and dust. That wasn't going to help her now any more than it had the last time she had seen him being hustled by his bodyguards into the limo, away from the carnage on the asphalt.

Senator Hartfer hadn't just voted for the American STEM Education Act. He had sponsored the bill. She shivered. Hartfer's beaming campaign-ad visage had graced the billboard outside her window until his reelection the previous November.

Her phone buzzed and her heart skipped a beat. Settle down Winkel. Just a text from James. She unlocked the phone.

"This is fucking bullshit," it said.

20

"No," said James. His hair flew from side to side as he shook his head. "We can't, Mara. We just can't."

"James," she said. "I don't like this anymore than you do."

It's insane." He threw up his hands. "It's fucking nuts. Why the hell would we replace Danielle with this Chad Zhukov guy? It makes no sense at all. No way."

It was just one thing after another. Like trying to assemble a puzzle in the middle of a tornado.

"He's eviscerating us." An abacus was evolving into a smartphone on James's t-shirt. "Danielle is our VP of Engineering. She's running three teams and four simultaneous implementations right now. We don't need this guy. It's going to hurt us, not help us."

Mara's knee ached from the fall last night and she could feel a migraine coming on. She looked over James's shoulder at the poster of Rocky Mountain National Park on the wall of her office. They would all need to channel that kind of mountain Zen to get through this.

Vernon crossed him arms. "James is right. It's not his place as a board member to do any of this. We're the management team. We're the ones saddled with riding Mozaik through the IPO rodeo. Our implementation queue is a mile long and it's growing every day. We need every ounce of expertise and knowhow we've got. It's hardly the time to replace Danielle."

"I'm not firing my fiancé," said James. "Lars is tearing apart our management team and reassembling it like a game of fucking Legos. It's a joke. A bad one."

"Enough." Mara held up her hands, silencing them. The migraine was rising like a full moon tide.

She dipped a hand into her pocket and grabbed her phone. She pressed a single finger to her lips and held it up in front of them. Then she popped off the back and removed the battery, placing both on the desk. James and Vernon followed suit although they didn't look happy about it. Mara ducked down and unplugged her computers' power cords from the outlet on the wall. She looked back and forth between them, holding eye contact for a few seconds.

"You think I want this?" she asked. "Our team is the most valuable asset we've built over the past year. We've all been busting our asses to ramp up to a point where we can actually serve the customers trampling each other to get through the door."

She laid her palm flat on the top of the folder. "This is bullshit, pure and simple," she said. "I know that. Both of you know that. I don't want a board member manipulating us. I don't want Lars sticking his dirty little fingers into Mozaik."

She raised her palm and then slapped it back onto the desk. James and Vernon jumped. "But unless either of you jockeys can make him disappear in an immediate and painful explosion, then what the fuck are we doing arguing about this?"

Standing, she pressed her fingertips against her temples. "Lars has made it very, very clear that we're to follow his instructions exactly. I'd be tempted to call his bluff and defy him, except that we already know the consequences. You're both right to hate his orders, but do we have any choice but to follow and resent them?"

She looked at James. "I know you don't want to fire Danielle. We'll create a new position for her, just like with Gordon. How about Chief Architect? I know the whole thing will piss her off but I'd rather have her mad than dead."

"What about Xavier? What about Special Task Force on Cyber Finance?" said James, clenching his jaw. "Aren't they supposed to be putting Lars in prison?"

"CyFi is running an investigation," said Mara. "We're a critical piece of that operation but assembling all the pieces could take years. They need to build an airtight case in order to put Lars away and deal a fatal blow to Maelstrom."

Vernon squeezed his eyes shut. "So you're saying we're on our own for this," he said.

Mara nodded.

"This is some bullshit," said James.

"Yep," said Mara, a knot forming in her stomach. "And we're going to douse it with maple syrup, smile, and pretend it tastes like buttermilk-fucking-pancakes."

21

MARA DODGED A LABRADOODLE PUPPY as she walked up Pearl Street. It had taken over a month to arrange this meeting. The intervening time had been filled with never-ending checklists and mountains of paperwork. It really shouldn't be called the "quiet period." Mozaik might not be able to make public announcements, but resolving the SEC comments on their S-1 made her meetings with the bankers and lawyers noisy and contentious. It had already been ten weeks since the board meeting, but it alternately felt like ten days or ten years.

Companies preparing to go public needed to start acting like publicly traded companies even before the IPO. That meant substantial formalization of Moziak's internal operations, recruiting new independent directors to their Board, rebuilding their financial reporting mechanisms from the bottom up, and lots and lots of lawyers. Watching the legal bills pile up, Mara wondered whether entrepreneurs or law firms benefited more when companies rang the bell on Wall Street.

But today she wasn't in New York. She was in Boulder, brushing shoulders with the geeks, hippies, and yuppies who called this little town home. Mara had fallen in love with the place as soon as she set foot on the CU campus, but its idyllic qualities clashed with the shadows she seemed to wrestle with every day. It was hard to play

Machiavelli with this many yoga studios all over the place.

Had she missed it? No. There was the sign, a sign featuring a stylized cow wearing a beret hung above the door. She stepped inside. A solid wood bar ran up one side of the room, customers clustered along it in groups. An electronic lounge remix of a classic swing album projected a relaxed, upbeat atmosphere. She made her way toward the back and found a free stool.

A large chalkboard displayed a list of featured milks. Each was delivered fresh from a variety of micro dairies around the American West. The staff's descriptions highlighted the floral accents in the milk from Marin County cows and the earthy mountain terroir from their cousins in alpine Colorado.

"Welcome to Milk Bar." The bartender, if that was the right word for him, had a waxed mustache and hair brushed straight back, 50s style. "What can I get for you?"

Mara chose at random. "Uhh, I've got a friend coming. Let's have two Oregon Coasts and a couple of cardamom walnuts."

He saluted her and turned to grab some glasses. He filled each with frothy milk from one of the taps along the wall behind the bar. Little tags described how they kept each keg at a slightly different temperature to complement the strengths of the particular draft. He placed each tall glass on a coaster in front of her with two large cookies on a white ceramic plate.

"Enjoy."

"Thanks." But he was already off to the other end of the bar to refill another customer's glass.

Mara broke off a piece of one of the cookies. It was still warm from the oven and the smell was making her mouth water. Yum. Then she sipped some of the much-touted milk, swished it around in her mouth like she was tasting a wine, and washed down the cookie.

"So, how is it?"

She looked up. Xavier looked tired behind his smile. His suit was rumpled and stubble peppered his chin.

"Good," she said. "I want to make fun of a bar that serves overpriced cookies and milk. But I have to admit, it's much better than anything you can find in a grocery store."

"These are the kind of innovations we just don't get back East," he said, collapsing onto a stool. "If I wanted fresh milk, I'd have to find a farm in Virginia." He took a sip and wiped his mouth with the back of a hand. "You're right. That's damn good."

The cookies didn't survive the small talk so they ordered more.

"So, you've been busy," he said.

"The road show starts next month," she said. "Any IPO is a lot of work. But when you're going as fast as we are, there isn't much time for this." She raised her new cookie and glass of milk, dunking the former into the latter. "I feel as tired as you look."

He sighed. "Too much time on a plane. I've been back and forth between San Francisco and DC too many times in the past few weeks."

Mara examined his face. The skin was smooth and clear, if a little pale. How much could she trust Xavier? Since they started collaborating, she hadn't held anything back from him.

"What has CyFi found out about Senator Hartfer?"

"Huh?" The question had clearly thrown him.

"Senator Hartfer. It's been more than a year since I reported what happened at that damn warehouse to you. What has CyFi turned up on him?"

"My area of investigation is Lars and Maelstrom directly," he said.

"Good for you," she said. "Now, answer my question."

"Well, I wish I had more to tell you. We initiated an investigation but the line of inquiry was shut down almost immediately."

She leaned forward. "What happened?"

"Nothing happened, that's what." He grimaced. "It came down

from way above my pay grade, no need to explore further. My team just kept working our other leads."

"So that's it?" She swept cookie crumbs off the bar with a hand. "You just accept it and move on? That's your level of due diligence?"

He grimaced. "I don't have a choice. That's the frustrating bit about working for the federal government. When I have orders, I obey them. There's a chain of command and the people sitting at the top aren't required to tell me what they're thinking."

Now it was Mara's turn to grimace. "You've got to do better than that," she said. "My family, friends, and employees are on the line here. This isn't some dry run simulation, this is the real thing. You want to hold us in limbo waiting for the right time to strike? That's your prerogative. But every time you come up empty when I ask you a question, I trust you less."

"I'm not lying," he said sharply.

"Did I say you were? I don't trust you less because I think you're being dishonest. I'm losing confidence in your ability to do what you say you're going to do, bring down Maelstrom. What progress have you made, exactly?"

"That's all classified. You know that." He looked pained.

"Enjoy your milk and cookies," she said. "It's appropriate to your level of professionalism." She stood and walked toward the door.

"Mara," Xavier called after her.

She didn't look back.

22

MARA STARED AT HER FACE in the mirror. Up close, she could see the new lines puckering around the corners of her eyes. Stress eroded people as surely as water did rock. Her cheekbones were sharper and her jaw more defined. Four months of preparation for the impending IPO had taken its toll. The cream white blouse stood in stark contrast to her mocha skin. A small jade pendant hung on a delicate silver chain around her neck.

Senator Hartfer had been meeting with Lars when Quinn had made his suicidal charge. Hartfer had sponsored the bill that made Mozaik a regulatory requirement. That bill essentially guaranteed that every bank on the planet needed Mozaik's services. Mozaik needed an enormous infusion of cash to buy companies like Larsons, AMQ, and Udemas so that they would have the staff to service the influx of new customers. The only way to access that amount of cash quickly enough was to go public. Lars had immediately delivered the IPO playbook to fast-track the process. Then he ordered them to replace Danielle with one of his own engineers, Chad. Oh, and she had blown off the only federal agent who was tasked with investigating the whole mess.

"Ahem."

Mara raised her eyes to the three people she could see reflected in their seats behind her.

Zach arched his elegant eyebrows. "What planet are you on?" he said. "Time for round three." His classic good looks appeared better suited to a centerfold than a conference room but he had proven to be a bloodhound in the hunt for potential institutional investors.

"You mean round five hundred and three," she said, sighing. She had been practicing the pitch four hours a day for the past two weeks. The script was invading her dreams and phrases from the spiel were wiggling their way into other conversations. This trio seemed intent on etching the words into her brain with a branding iron. She knew it was necessary, but that didn't make it any less grinding.

"No room for slipups," said Leslie, whom, they had discovered, lacked any sense of humor. She adjusted her pen a fraction of an inch to align with the top of her legal pad. "The road show starts tomorrow and Mozaik is liable for every single thing you say. It needs to be perfect every time."

"When we're actually pitching, we'll play a game," said Grant, lifting his chin. "Who can work the word 'moist' into their pitch as many times as possible? Loser buys the winner their choice of single malt."

"You're on," said Mara, her lips split into a smile. "I bet your armpits are getting moist just thinking about the level of competition I'm going to bring to the table."

Grant pressed two fists together and flexed his biceps. His muscles made it look like weasels were mating under his shirt. "Give me all you got," he said.

Leslie frowned at Grant. "Let's get on with it," she said.

Mara closed her eyes and took a breath. When she opened them, she smiled and dove straight into the speech. It was second nature now. She had practiced by herself, in front of a group, a camera, a mirror. She couldn't remember how many times they'd been over it with a fine-toothed comb.

The pitch covered the canned story arc of Mozaik from its founding through to its current status. Then it delved into the future prospects for the company, focusing on the opportunities based on the provisions of the American STEM Education Act. Every sentence was engineered to paint a compelling, lucrative, legally defensible picture of Mozaik.

As she fell into the natural rhythm of the presentation, her thoughts began to wander. Had she been wrong to walk out on Xavier? After all, he was just doing his job and they were on the same side. Without him, they were just a couple of pawns in Lars's game. But working with him had made her feel like nothing more than a pawn of CyFi. As if that hadn't been frustrating enough, CyFi hadn't demonstrated much real progress. She understood that investigations might take a long time. That's exactly what she had said to James and Vernon. But she couldn't swallow how quickly Xavier had brushed off her question about Senator Hartfer. It was the cherry on top of a fraught partnership.

Mara jerked back and her hands flew up. Leslie was snapping her fingers an inch in front of Mara's nose.

"Get with the program Winkel," she said, pinching her lips together. "IPOs don't sell themselves."

Grant snickered and stage whispered to Zach, "Guess who's got moist armpits now?"

23

"TO OUR FEARLESS LEADER, may she return with booty and plunder for all." Vernon flashed a dashing smile and raised his tumbler. In the fleeting moments when their little cohort got together, he always seemed to play the role of beneficent host. That quality had translated over from his life as a DJ, and now served him well running Mozaik's partnerships.

"I'm the dancing monkey, remember?" said Mara, shimmying and making an orangutan face as she raised her glass to join the others. James had his arm draped over Danielle's shoulder and the four of them were crammed into a secluded booth at the Mountain Sun Pub on Pearl Street. "It's like a way bigger version of our Series A."

"You'll get it done," said Danielle, deliberate and serious. She had taken the bump to Chief Architect gracefully but Mara still harbored a knot of impotent frustration at being forced into inserting Chad as their VP of Engineering.

"What exactly is the point of this specific part of the monkey dance, again?" James swiped the hair out of his eyes. "It seems ridiculous how much time Zach and Grant have forced you to spend practicing."

Vernon shook his head in mock astonishment. "And we call you our resident genius..."

Danielle poked James with an elbow and said, "He's good with math but you'd be amazed how the house keys seem to evade his impressive intellect."

James pecked Danielle with a kiss on the cheek that she unsuccessfully tried to dodge. "We all have our strengths," he said. "And those keys are sneaky bastards."

Mara laughed and sipped her beer. She was hyped up with tension from the endless preparation but if she could ever truly relax, it was with the people around this table. She appreciated their obvious effort to salve her frayed nerves.

Vernon took a long pull from his tumbler and held up a finger for James's attention. "The road show is Mara's opportunity to woo major institutional investors to preorder shares in Mozaik's IPO." He inclined his head to her. "Mara sells them on our glittering future and incomparable prospects. Zach and his team record their orders in The Book. The Book determines our stock price on opening day and the success of our public offering. So yeah, it's a pretty important pirouette."

"Basically, it's a nonstop schmooze session with a bunch of really, really rich folks," said Mara, smiling wryly.

James held up his hands. "Ugh," he said. "Thank the gods I don't have to come along for the ride."

"If you did, investors would run for the hills and The Book would fall limp into Zach's hands," said Vernon with a faux glare. "They're generally not fans of cute t-shirts." He gestured to James's chest, which displayed a cartoon thought bubble filled with Hadoop code. "That's why Mara gets to take point on this one."

"Huzzah," said Mara. "See the sacrifices I make for the team?"

"What a martyr," said Vernon. "Life on a private jet sure is tough."

Mara drained her glass. "Speaking of, I gotta go pack."

"Duty calls," said Vernon, nodding. "I need to review the due diligence documents from Ken Li over at Larsons."

After settling the tab, they stood and made for the door. Mara paused to take a breath of fresh evening air as they split up to walk to their various apartments. Vernon strode purposely away. He had grown to fill a major part of their leadership team, especially since Quinn's untimely death. James and Danielle sauntered off hand in hand in the other direction. Mara had never seen James so content. He still worked as hard as ever but something had definitely changed. He was more buoyant, less obsessive. Danielle had grown more flexible, more resilient. She still had the same razor-sharp brilliance, but now she even made the occasional joke.

Mara ran a hand through her hair, and looked up at the stars glimmering through the haze of city glow. Surrounded by so much uncertainty, danger, and confusion, it was a blessing to have true friends at her side.

24

MARA SUNK INTO HER LEATHER SEAT as the Gulfstream G650 taxied to the runway. She had to make an effort to keep her foot from tapping. Nervous energy had suffused her body for the past week.

In four days they had already visited Denver, San Francisco, L.A., Chicago, Houston, Boston, and New York. Mara would eat a granola bar as they rushed from a private airfield to a breakfast meeting. Zach would introduce them to the attending investors. She had fourteen minutes to present the strategic portion of the pitch and then Grant spent seven minutes going through the financials. Then they would suck down stale coffee and field questions. Always conscious of the schedule, Zach would herd them into the waiting car and they would burn rubber en route to the inevitable rubber chicken lunch meeting. Then, it was back to the airfield, and onto the next city for a dinner pitch. Rinse. Repeat.

Kicking off her shoes, she scrunched her toes into the thick carpet. She felt like some kind of business rock star. Zipping around the country on a private jet. Ushered from place to place in a limo by a banker in a three-piece suit. With so many high-powered pitches back-to-back, the background buzz of caffeine and adrenaline never left her.

Mozaik was on tour. Zach was her warm-up band. She was the main act and Grant was her closer. She could hear the two of them talking in quiet tones up at the front of the plane. They were probably going over what the current count on The Book was. That was the whole point of the road show, whipping up interest in buying their stock in the run up to the IPO.

The people on the other side of the mediocre lunches were worth billions of dollars. They ran hedge funds, family offices, private equity groups, and financial institutions. It was different than pitching angel investors or venture capitalists. These guys, and they were almost all *guys*, didn't care about technological promise or opportunities to create new markets. All they cared about was Mozaik's financial profile and finding ways to outsmart their peers. Zach was great at playing them against each other to generate a sense of urgency, but Mara found the whole thing vaguely depressing. It was so mundane, so zero sum.

She rubbed at her neck with the heel of her hand. Her throat was sore from so much talking. James would have hated all this theater, but she missed having him here. It felt odd for him to be absent during all these pitches, but CTOs rarely participated in roadshows. Plus, she needed him focused on leading the team back in Boulder. The amount of work needed to prepare for the post-IPO worldwide rollout was hard to fathom. Getting ready for it with a new, investor-imposed VP of Engineering was even more daunting.

The engines roared, and the acceleration pushed her back into her seat. Private jets made 747s seem like bumbling public buses. She could get used to traveling this way.

Regardless, she'd be seeing James on Tuesday for all the final meetings in New York before they rang the bell on Wall Street next Thursday. Their families would be coming out as well, plus their board members, and a number of Mozaik employees. In the meantime, she needed to make this road show a success. As Zach said approximately seventeen times a day, "Don't schmooze? You lose."

Mara pressed her nose against the extra-large window and watched the lights of Manhattan fall away beneath them. With her confidence in Xavier and CyFi slipping, it was up to her to make the most out of this mess. They couldn't afford to continue outsourcing the solution. She had to find a way to undermine Lars and his plans without putting their loved ones in danger.

From this altitude it seemed a world away. Billionaire gangsters playing at venture capital sounded like the premise to a bad spy movie, not the flesh-and-blood motherfuckers who had waltzed in to ruin her life. But then she remembered the soulless look on Maria's face at Quinn's funeral and the lingering hope that this could all be a delusion imploded into stark reality.

If she wanted to take Lars down on her own terms, she needed resources. Resources that went far beyond what were available to her as a startup founder on Walnut Street. That's where the IPO came in.

What had started as a pure business opportunity for Mozaik had evolved into a critical move in the game against Maelstrom. She had a good team of people around her, at least some of whom she could trust. Going public would put so much cash in the bank that they wouldn't know what to do with it. They would cement the acquisitions of Udemas, Larsons, and AMQ. Vernon had been quietly advancing the deals. With their expert teams in hand, they would roll out Mozaik to every major bank on Earth. The IPO would diversify their investor base and create more transparency, both of which would loosen Lars's hold on them. As the CEO of a successful public company, she would be on more even footing with Lars. She could order things in a heartbeat that right now she could only dream of. She would have the levers and reach to strike back and make it hurt. Make it permanent.

"Four 'moists' in one pitch, impressive Winkel. The Force is strong with this one."

Mara snapped back to the present and looked up. Grant stood in front of her, one hand on the back of her chair and the other holding a tumbler of amber liquid. He had taken off his tie and loosened his collar. Zach appeared by his side and wrapped an arm around his shoulders.

"I told this guy he had no chance against you." Zach grinned. "His frat boy confidence can't compete with the cold steel of your relentless determination."

"We came over to rouse you from your hermitage," said Grant. "You look in need of a stiff drink."

"How's The Book looking?" asked Mara. Her sense of humor wasn't rising to the occasion.

"See?" Zach turned to Grant. "Relentless."

"Good," said Grant. "But not good enough for us to get sloppy."

"It will *never* be good enough for you to get sloppy," said Zach.

"Sloppiness isn't my style," she said. "Zach, can you please have the pilot reroute the plane to D.C.? There's someone I need to see before we do the rounds in Atlanta."

Zach's grin vanished. "Impossible. That will throw off the entire schedule."

She stared at him until it was uncomfortable, and then waited an extra five seconds. "I have full confidence in your ability to achieve the impossible," she said. "That confidence is why I'm trusting you with our IPO. Don't worry. We'll fill The Book. I expect us to be at least twenty times oversubscribed." She smiled. "But we will be stopping in D.C."

She turned back to the window. Outside, the running lights intermittently illuminated the claustrophobic womb of a fog bank. Long games required long plays.

25

A SMALL BELL TINKLED as Mara stepped inside. The Lebanese market smelled of roasting meat, coffee, and frankincense. Colorful imported food crowded the rows of shelves. An employee was restocking the fresh produce section and a row of gaudy hookahs sat along the wall, price tags dangling.

Mara walked over into the food service side of the market. White plastic tables and chairs sat out in front of the open kitchen and grill. A spit of shawarma spun lazily and the refrigerated glass case below the counter displayed everything from baba ganoush to baklava. Little placards named each dish in Arabic, French, and English.

She approached the counter, ordered enough food for two people, and found a seat at a table in the corner. They wouldn't have a lot of time this morning. Zach would be fretting over the schedule right now, probably burning up bandwidth yelling at various executive assistants.

The bell jingled again and she looked up. Juliana stepped through the door, eyes searching the market. She wore a conservative business suit that set off her dark hair and bronze skin.

Juliana spotted her and walked over to the table. "Hello, Mara," said Juliana. "Definitely a different atmosphere than our last meeting."

Mara stood and shook her hand. "This place has great reviews online," she said. "And I figured you could probably use a break from the White House."

"The Mess isn't known for its falafel," said Juliana, sitting down. "But I'm assuming you didn't come all the way to D.C. for the ethnic cuisine."

Mara held up a piece of pita topped with a generous dollop of labneh. "After the endless rounds of corporate cooking I've been devouring this week, a hole-in-the-wall like this is a rare treat."

Juliana laughed and scooped up a forkful of fattoush. "I've been following the news of your road show. Sounds like you're drumming up quite a bit of interest. Next week will be exciting for Mozaik."

Mara nodded. "I try not to count my chickens, but it's going well so far."

They both ate in silence for a moment, savoring the liberal garlic and parsley. Mara watched Juliana. The gray in her hair lent a sense of gravity to her intensity. They had never grown close, but the tightness in Mara's stomach loosened a bit. Here was someone she could trust.

Reaching into her pocket, Mara withdrew her cell phone. She placed it on the table, popped off the case, and removed the battery. Then she looked up at Juliana, and took a long sip of fresh mint lemonade.

Juliana cocked her head to the side and frowned. Then she pulled her phone from her purse and did the same.

"Sometimes it's hard to find the line between caution and paranoia," said Mara, quirking her mouth to the side. "But I prefer to be careful."

"So, is this why I'm getting my dose of shawarma?" asked Juliana. "No snoops at the neighborhood Lebanese market."

Mara shrugged. "Better safe than sorry."

Juliana wiped her mouth with a napkin and leaned forward.

"Now that the little birds aren't listening, maybe you can tell me what is so important that you made a last minute stop in Washington in the middle of your IPO road show."

Mara finished the last of her lemonade and took a deep breath. "The higher you go, the more people you find whose priority is to get even higher," she said. "You told me that before we painted a target on Morris and McLeay."

Juliana nodded. "I remember. I was explaining why I couldn't take the investigation to my bosses. It was too big to fail. Schemes of that scale find traction in places you can't anticipate and the people at the top have the most to lose."

"Well," said Mara. "We're in the middle of an investigation that may be larger than the DVG scandal. It involves an old colleague of McLeay. In fact, we believe that the man in question orchestrated McLeay's downfall so that he could fill the resulting power vacuum. We had hoped to nail this guy with the DVG probe, but he set up McLeay instead." She shivered, remembering Lars's flat gaze.

Air hissed through Juliana's teeth as she exhaled. "I always wondered why Quinn walked out of the room when Mozaik revealed Morris and McLeay's culpability."

Mara's eyes widened, surprised that Juliana remembered that moment. "Yes," said Mara. "That's right. Overall the sting was a resounding success. We were thrilled to see the software doing its job. But we knew there were still bigger fish in the sea."

"And so, now you're organizing a deep sea fishing trip."

"In a way, yes," said Mara. "After the DVG news broke, I was approached by an agent from the Special Task Force for Cyber Finance."

"CyFi."

"I didn't know —"

"I wouldn't be much of a financial reform czar if I didn't know about a program like that." Juliana's face had become very still.

"And if they're involved, then this must be a very large fish indeed." She tapped her denuded phone with an index finger.

"Of course." They were both silent for a moment. Lebanese pop music washed over them. One of the cooks was singing along. They had arrived well before the lunch rush and other customers were only now starting to filter in.

"So far, we've been cooperating fully with CyFi." Mara bit the inside of her cheek.

"But?"

"But I'm worried they may be compromised in some way," said Mara in a rush.

"In what way?" asked Juliana, her gaze flicking around the room.

"When we raided DVG, you waited until the last minute to coordinate. Even then, you only reached out to middle managers, boots on the ground folks. I suspect that the rank and file at CyFi are doing their best. But it feels like the investigation is stalling, and upper management has been inserting itself into operations."

"Never a good sign," said Juliana. "Corruption tends to trickle down from the top. The folks in the trenches have to face the reality of criminality every day. They're harder to sway and slower to rationalize wrongdoing. Plus, as I said last time, they tend to have less at stake."

"Right," said Mara. "But that's an unorthodox approach. You had days of phone calls after DVG where this or that director or under-secretary screamed themselves hoarse threatening to put your head on a platter."

"Bluster and bullshit," said Juliana. "In my experience, the best way to fix the system is not to trust it in the first place."

"And that," said Mara, "is exactly why I made this little detour." She crumpled her napkin in a fist and tossed it onto the table. Zach was probably nearing cardiac arrest out in the car, but she felt better than she had since walking out on Xavier. It was good to be actually doing something instead of wasting away in the wings. "I don't know when, where, or how. But I do know that one way or another, I will need your help on this fishing expedition."

26

MARA SIPPED ON A GRAPEFRUIT JUICE and stared at the videoconference screen. Pages of notes covered the polished walnut table in front of her and Zach and Grant sat on either side. The Gulfstream was packed with luxurious accoutrements, making the geeky hipster themes of their office in Boulder seem adolescent by comparison.

Mara concealed a smile as she ran a fingertip along the smooth wood. She'd take Boulder over private jets any day. The conservative lines and overstocked minibars called up images of oligarchs whose wealth was outsized only by their egos. At least her team didn't take themselves so seriously. They had the grace to fetishize comic book heroes instead of big game hunting.

"We've been forced to settle both lawsuits."

Mara's attention snapped back to the screen. This was the last leadership standup call before the final meeting tomorrow in New York where they finalized IPO pricing with Zach and his team. Leslie had been summarizing their efforts to wrap up all the open legal questions.

"I missed that last," said Mara. "Why did we settle?"

"The first was from a job applicant who wasn't selected for the position in question," said Leslie. "He's a forty-two-year-old engineer who's claiming we discriminated against him because of age. He's pointing to the average age of our engineering team as evidence."

Leslie flipped over a page on her legal pad. "The second is a trademark issue. A group, claiming to have subsidiary name rights to the original Mosaic browser from the early nineties, says that we're in violation because we haven't paid them for use of the name."

"But we spell it with a 'z' and a 'k'," said James, the image switching to his face as soon as he started talking. "Marc Andreessen wrote that software when he was still working at NCSA. It was awesome. It popularized the web. That's why we named it Mozaik Industries in the first place. Hopefully, we'll be able to democratize finance."

"Both of those claims are utter bullshit," said Mara, sitting up in her chair.

"Nuisance suits," Grant said in a bored voice.

"That's right," said Leslie, the screen shifting back to her. "Neither suit has a leg to stand on in court."

"But we can't let them go to court, we'd have to disclose them to SEC and our potential stock buyers," said Zach.

"They're trolls," said James.

"They know we're going public, and we can't afford disclosures," said Leslie. "They're extorting us for money because it's obvious we'll have to settle. There are lawyers whose entire job is just this. It comes up in virtually every IPO. Nothing to worry about."

"I don't like getting mugged," said Mara. She glanced over at Grant's spreadsheets. It was unbelievable how quickly this IPO was draining Mozaik's coffers.

"Going public is the corporate equivalent of walking around in a dangerous neighborhood by yourself while texting on the newest iPhone," said Leslie. "No way to get around it but to pay. Disclosures would cost us far more by impacting our price point."

Mara clenched her teeth. "Alright, who's next?"

"I've got some good news," said Sue, beaming under her crown of brown curls. "Obviously, our IPO is generating a lot of media interest. We've got the usual pile of coverage lined up. But I just got off the phone with the general manager at *Hedrick's Report*. They want you back on, Mara. They agreed to send their entire team to New York and record a live interview with you, right before you ring the opening bell at the New York Stock Exchange. It's a coup for them and us."

Mara smiled. "Are you going to give me a hard time about sticking to my notes this time?"

"You bet your foul mouth I am," said Sue with a mock stern look. "Working with you is like media coaching a goat."

"A moist goat?" asked Grant.

"No points," said Zach. "That was totally lame."

James swiped the hair from in front of his eyes. "As I was drinking my coffee this morning, I realized there's something we need to go over together, Mara. It's a little in the weeds so we can take the conversation offline."

Mara frowned and did a double take on James. His t-shirt featured a stylized green python engaged in an epic battle with a flashing red ruby. James was an oolong aficionado and could taste the difference between grades of sencha. He probably drank five cups of tea a day. He never drank coffee. While they were still working from coffee shops, he had always complained that although the baristas would go to great lengths to prepare esoteric espresso concoctions, it was all but impossible to get the temperature right for each tea varietal. His face didn't betray anything. Mara couldn't help but wonder what detailed technical problem could possibly require so much input from her that it would require a dedicated follow-up meeting?

"Okay," said Mara before the silence became awkward. "Why don't we deal with it in New York, tomorrow evening." Was that a flicker of frustration that had just passed over James's face? What other options did they have? If this was something so sensitive that he wanted to hide it from the people in the meeting, and didn't want to just call her individually, then they would have to go over it in person.

Vernon picked up the slack. "Good news on the empire building front. AMQ's CEO has tacit approval from his board on the acquisition. Once things get official, there will be quite a bit of haggling over price, just like with Larsons and Udemas. But having them notionally on board means the transition should be smoother. That's the third jewel in our crown. With them, we'll have enough manpower to service all our major clients. The banks are happy about it too. They already work with them anyway so it's just adding a new layer to their workflow."

"We're ready to go on technical rollout with 80 percent of the major banks," said James. "We can press 'go' as soon as we have the additional staff on board from AMQ, Larsons, and Udemas to support deployment."

"Great," said Zach. "I'll pass that little tidbit along to my team. During this final window, we want all signs pointing onward and upward. Nothing makes a bidding war bloodier than a hot prospect getting hotter." There was something feral in his grin that made Mara appreciate that she hadn't had to go through the banker selection process herself.

"It's full steam ahead on this end," said Grant. "We'll do the final rundown tomorrow during the pricing meeting. For now, we just need to keep our eyes on the ball for the last few pitches."

"Ten minutes to landing in Charlotte." The pilot's voice came over the P.A. system.

Mara took the last swig of grapefruit juice. "Alright folks. Let's wrap this up and get to work."

They were on the final lap. She needed to keep up her energy level for the sprint. This is when singular focus made all the difference.

She opened the file on the hedge fund manager they were flying to North Carolina to meet. But even as she went over his background, she couldn't set aside the incongruous mental image of James drinking a cappuccino.

27

"THANK YOU, FOLKS." Zach plucked the glass in front of him that an assistant had just topped up with champagne. "Road shows are never without speed bumps, but we knocked the ball out of the park on this one. Lars, we really appreciate you bringing this deal to us in the first place." Lars raised a self-deprecating hand from his seat next to David and the new independent board members. "Major kudos to Grant for distilling the numbers and Leslie for tightening up the legal angles." He nodded down the table at them.

"But most of all," Zach raised his glass, "thank you to Mara and the entire team for building such a valuable company. Two days from now Mozaik will be taking its rightful place among the great businesses of our generation. You guys are changing the world, and we're all going to make a lot of money helping you do it."

Everyone chuckled, raised their glasses, and took a sip of champagne. This was the largest conference room Mara had ever been in. Its level of opulence made the Gulfstream look like an air taxi with bad makeup. Twenty-five people sat around an oval mahogany table the size of a small solar system. Decanters of ice water, fresh squeezed orange juice, and scotch were sprinkled along its length.

"Now, if you'll excuse me," said Zach, half bowing. "We've got a deal that's thirty-four times oversubscribed and there are orders to book." The bankers leapt up from their seats and made straight for the doors. Mara had noticed them checking their phones during the entire pricing discussion.

Now that the main event was over, the room was fragmenting into half a dozen different side conversations.

"Good work boss," said Vernon, squeezing her shoulder. "After seeing you go off-book during the TechPitch presentation in San Diego, I knew the road show was going to be a cinch for you."

"Let's hope it yields better results than TechPitch did." A memory flashed by. Her feet dangling out over the water as she looked at the sparkling running lights of an aircraft carrier over the dark bay.

Vernon laughed. "It sounds like that won't be a problem. I've rarely heard bankers be that bullish on the eve of an offering. And anyway, you met me at TechPitch. Isn't that enough of a silver lining for you?"

She allowed herself a smile, heaving a theatrical sigh. "And now I have a DJ running corporate development."

"Oh, you don't fool me," said Vernon. "I know you love to be the life of the party."

"Well, she's certainly the life of the party today," said David, joining them. His wild hair, wool sweater, and Birkenstocks stuck out from the crowd of custom cufflinks. "Mara, I'm incredibly proud of you." He raised his glass. "Two years ago you were struggling to scrape together some seed money. Now," he opened his arms wide to encompass the room, "you're the hottest deal on Wall Street. You want to know my favorite part about the whole thing?" He glanced over both shoulders. "How excited these guys are about a technology that will probably reshape the entire financial industry. They're so focused on their big payday that they don't see how much Mozaik might directly impact their own jobs."

"Thanks, David," said Mara. "That means a lot coming from you. You were the person who stepped up to the plate for us during our seed round. We wouldn't be here today if it weren't for you." She had been plagued by fears of having to abandon Mozaik to seek employment at Starbucks or crawl back to her parents to ask for help. They were sticking to their original range. By Thursday afternoon, Mozaik would have two hundred million dollars cash in the bank and she and James would each be worth one hundred and seventy million dollars on paper. The numbers were too big to fathom. She had been ferried directly to this conference room in Manhattan, after the airplane landed earlier this afternoon. She was still riding the road show adrenaline high. The world was a carnival built of anxiety and anticipation.

David's eyes twinkled. "When are your families getting in?"

"They'll arrive tomorrow afternoon," said Mara, thinking of her parents back in California. She had tried to see them between pitches in L.A., but the timing hadn't worked out. It was going to be weird seeing them both in the same room again. She hadn't seen them together since that fateful sushi dinner at Osaka when she told them she was dropping out of college. James's family was coming out too although Danielle was staying in Boulder with Chad to ensure that everything continued smoothly in their absence. "That way they can join for the big breakfast at the New York Stock Exchange on Thursday morning before we ring the bell. That reminds me, I need to talk to James."

She turned away, looking for him. He shouldn't be hard to find. James was the only person besides David not wearing a suit. His t-shirt featured a print of the original *Star Wars* 1977 theatrical poster.

Mara wanted to ask him about his comment during the videoconference yesterday morning. What was so important that he needed to tell her about it but couldn't do it virtually? She also needed to update him on Xavier and her meeting with Juliana. They would need to go over the details of their long-term plan together.

After the IPO and acquisitions settled out, they would have some serious weight to throw at Maelstrom. But she couldn't see him through the clusters of people.

"Ms. Winkel." The quiet voice sliced through her thoughts and raised the hair on the back of her neck. She had been carefully avoiding Lars since arriving earlier this afternoon. As an investor and board member, he was involved in this last flurry of activity leading up to the offering. But that didn't mean she wanted to interact with him. Steeling herself, she turned to face him.

His pale eyes were flint gray. "Congratulations on running quite the road show," he said.

"Thank you," she said, nodding stiffly.

"There are a few small things I'd like chat with you about and Zach has assured me that you don't have any formal obligations this evening."

"I have a lot to go over with my team," said Mara. "I'm sure you understand."

"But of course," said Lars, with a tight lipped smile. "You will have more than enough time for that. But first, there is something I simply must show you."

28

COLD SWEAT POURED AROUND THE HOLSTER at Mara's back. She shouldn't be here. Lars's limo had whisked them from the bank to a glass and steel edifice of Manhattan luxury condos. She hadn't wanted to leave with him. Hadn't wanted to get in the car with him. Didn't want to be here right now. But what choice did she have? Her gut might rebel but he held the ultimate cards. Would she risk the safety of her friends and family simply to avoid being alone with him? What would her refusal accomplish?

Lars pulled his key from the slot and the elevator doors opened onto polished marble. The apartment must cover the entire floor. The open design was all high ceilings, natural light, and minimalism. It made Mara think of a flock of starlings taking flight.

She could only imagine the extravagant expense lavished on this place. Original modern artwork hung on purpose built walls and the rising notes from an orchestral performance trickled from an invisible but omnipresent sound system.

Lars gestured and she stepped out of the elevator, followed by him and one of the minders that never left his side. Lars murmured something to him and the man nodded and moved off down a corridor to the right.

Now she was alone with the mastermind behind Maelstrom, the man who had orchestrated the deaths of Craig, Quinn and so many others. Should she pull the pistol and shoot him in the face while she had the chance? No. She needed a key to operate the elevator and her gun had no silencer. His minion would charge in within seconds and she'd be as good as dead.

"Come," said Lars, the heels of his shoes clicking on the marble as he strode ahead. He wore a tailored gray suit under his long wool coat. "There's no excuse to miss a clear winter sunset in New York City."

She needed to be smart. What would Xavier do in this position? She might be sick and tired of CyFi's lack of initiative, but his entire job revolved around navigating situations like this. Even if his strategic assistance was questionable, she could sure use his tactical help right now.

Xavier would look at her present position as an opportunity, not a risk. Lars had invited her here for a reason. She would make a note of the address on her way out. Maybe this was his home, his inner sanctum. Or maybe it was a goddamn Airbnb. There was no way to tell. But as she followed Lars, she tried to memorize the layout of the place and note as many details as possible.

She would gather as much intelligence as she could. Data like this was what they needed in order to figure out what Maelstrom was really up to. The more they knew, the less likely they'd paint themselves into a corner. They had fucked up the DVG sting by assuming superiority and playing inside Lars's lines. Their arrogance had made them easy to manipulate.

Craig had made the same mistake. Playing detective when he had no clue what was really going on. They had been in over their heads before even dipping their feet in the pool. All of them had been too clever for their own good.

They approached the side of the apartment opposite the elevator doors. The entire wall was a glass window overlooking Manhattan. Lars clapping his hands once, a surprisingly delicate gesture, and the entire sheet of glass split down the middle and slid open.

They stepped out onto the wide patio beyond. Another waist-high wall of glass served as the railing. Mara was glad she had kept her coat. Lars had too. The evening air of a January in New York was bracing, or, more accurately, frigid. She stuffed her hands into her pockets.

"How rude," said Lars, turning back inside. "I forgot the important part." Mara let him go and used the moment of solitude to try to bring her heart rate back down to something approximating normal.

A minute later, Lars was back with two tulip glasses of amber liquid.

"D'Esperance," he said, passing one to her. His bold Scandinavian features made him look more like a downhill skiing champion than an organized crime boss. "The only Armagnac brandy worth drinking. A vista like this demands it."

The view from the balcony was stunning. The setting sun threw long shadows over the patchwork of long Manhattan avenues, hulking skyscrapers, and snowy roofs. Golden hour light made exposed brick walls appear to glow from within and transformed the urban jungle into a postcard.

Lars waved a hand. "This is why I bought the place. Too gorgeous to pass up." He shrugged. "The selling agent knew what he was doing, he arranged a 5:30 p.m. walk-through. I was annoyed until I saw the sunset. Then I had to have it. My photographer friends go green with envy."

"It's beautiful," said Mara, she couldn't argue with that.

"But I'm getting ahead of myself," he said, raising his Armagnac. "To Mozaik, may she root out the scum of this Earth and make us rich beyond our wildest dreams."

The brandy was rich. Floral notes danced over the smoldering heat of the alcohol. The burning in the back of her throat was welcome in the chill. She shook her head, staring out over the forest of buildings.

"Is it not to your liking?" asked Lars. "I can have François open a different bottle."

"No, the brandy's fine," said Mara. Something shifted inside her. If she was stuck here, she might as well make the most of it. "It's just... why?"

"Because you shook your head, I assumed it was the drink."

"No, not that," she said. "Why... all this? Why bring me up here? Why ply me with views and toasts? When others are present, posturing makes sense. You can't risk anyone catching on to whatever you're really up to. But you've been holding a guillotine over my head for over a year now. So why beat around the bush?"

"Mara, Mara." The light caught his face in profile as he swiveled his head to face her. "Subtlety never was your specialty."

He pursed his lips and exhaled. "You misunderstand me," he said. "Truly, you do."

"What?" asked Mara. It might be dangerous to be so direct but it felt damn good after all this time. "Do you have an orphan sob story for me to justify being a ruthless mobster? Is that why we're here? Because you want me to sympathize with your plight and admire your real estate? Empathy can be tough for victims of your own blackmail."

"Everyone has a story." His voice was quiet, just on the edge of hearing above the noise from the traffic so many floors below. "But I'm not looking for sympathy from anyone. My father ran operations for Heckerman."

"The defense contractor?"

"Hah," he said. "That's what the politicians call it. Heckerman is a private army-for-hire. As soon as I was old enough to shoot, he brought me along to see how the world really worked." His face hardened. "Somalia. Nicaragua. Lebanon. Congo. It was a better education than any platinum plated prep school, I can tell you that much. All these damn kids scramble through the Ivy League with raging hard-ons for power. They end up working on the Hill, or on Wall Street, or even Silicon Valley."

He spat over the edge of the balcony. "They don't know shit. They mistake the trappings for the real thing. They think that justice is something that institutions define and that governments exist to empower people. It's pathetic. Institutions are meaningless. Governments equally so. Nothing but human fabrication."

Holding up his tulip glass, he gazed at the liquid rendered molten by rays of setting sun. "Organizations are means of control. They are tools, org charts. They delineate the execution of power, they are not its origin. When your Boulder hippies claim that corporations want to replace the US Government, they're dead wrong. True power brokers *outsource governance to governments* so they don't have to manage the headaches of a monstrous bureaucracy. Real power is personal. Real power is knowing another man's secret. Real power is relationships." His eyes snapped back to her. "And there is real power in our relationship."

A shudder went through Mara's body as if the winter chill had sent a finger down the back of her jacket. She thought of the manila envelope with its cargo of glossy terror and remembered the taste of vomit. She sipped her brandy to give her a moment to gather herself. "Are you referring to your ever-so-sweet care package?"

"Do I look like an insurance salesman?" He shook his head, frustrated.

"What?"

"Your care package of family photos is an insurance policy, nothing more. Leverage is required to build a serious organization. I certainly wouldn't be building this kind of partnership with you without holding a few cards in reserve."

An insurance policy, that's how he justified holding her loved ones lives hostage. She wanted to pistol whip him in the face and push him over the balcony. But she'd still have to get out of this penthouse hellhole. Forcing the anger down, she tried to focus on what she could actually learn here.

"So," she said. "When you say our relationship holds real power, do you mean the IPO? Obviously, we're going to be making Maelstrom a lot of money. You'll be able to afford a few more views like this." She gestured at the purpling sky.

"Pffft." He raised a hand and waved away her comment like a fly. "Venture capitalists call going public an exit but it's a beginning, not an end. We're holding our position in Mozaik. The paper value will skyrocket of course, which is always good to see. But it's a drop in the bucket. No, I didn't get to where I am today by hitting singles. The beauty of operating in the background is that you aren't subject to the petty whims of stakeholders or oversight. It gives you the freedom to make long bets."

He looked off into the distance for a moment. The sun was just starting to dip under the horizon. "Wallis couldn't see that," he said. "Among other things. That's why I so deeply appreciated your assistance removing him from the game. He opposed investing in you in the first place, can you imagine? Some laggards just can't see how technology is eating their comfortable little world out from under them. Innovations like Mozaik reshape the playing field. It's a bet worth making. It's a relationship worth forging."

"Then what do you want from us, from me?" Her fist clenched around the glass and Mara had to struggle not to scream the words. They had targeted Lars with their DVG sting but he had diverted the blow to oust his rival, Wallis. Everything he said made her feel like a tool.

Lars stared at her frankly, as if the answer was obvious. "Ms. Winkel, you have made yourself a critical piece in this puzzle. My partners and I, at Maelstrom, manage the wealth, created by many entrepreneurs around the world, who value absolute discretion. We are their bankers, lawyers, lobbyists, advisers, and confidantes. We stop at nothing to maximize shareholder value, and do right by our clients."

Mara snorted. "I've never heard money laundering described in those terms before. Who are your clients? Dictators? Drug lords? Arms dealers? Corrupt politicians?" She could hardly believe she was being this brazen with him. But what did she have to lose? He knew she was in no position to add bite to her bark right now. She could only hope that with the IPO in the bag, she'd be able to orchestrate a more meaningful opposition.

Lars's voice turned hard. "When I say absolute discretion, I mean it. We see the world for what it truly is and serve those who choose to throw down the gauntlet instead of letting life float by behind rose tinted lenses. Realpolitik is what it sounds like."

"You haven't answered my question." She didn't need to hear any more dystopian rationalizations.

"But of course." Lars sipped his brandy. A siren wailed somewhere far below. The last bright edge of sun disappeared beyond a distant skyscraper.

"Mozaik is the key," said Lars. "At first, I thought it was little more than a toy. A thorn in my side. But its ability to coax signal from the noise of the financial whirlwind makes it indispensable to those arbiters of capitalism that live in this fine city. They just didn't know it yet. That's why I had Donald pass the STEM Act. Now, they simply *must* have it. The banks have been begging the White House for concrete financial security guidelines, for years. That law makes Mozaik the gold star that absolves them from liability. No banking executive on Earth can afford *not* to implement your software."

"And that," he said, finishing his brandy. "Is what brings us to the present moment. Here in the beating heart of the free market, the cutting edge of commerce. This is where royalty is made. You may call me a robber baron but history is written by the victors. And you, Mara Winkel, have a very important part to play in this little coup. Mozaik is my Trojan Horse."

29

COLOR FADED FROM THE SKY, and lights blinked to life in the ocean of buildings before them. Mara didn't know how to respond to Lars's soliloquy. She emptied her glass of brandy. The sweetness was cloying, and the liquor burned the back of her throat. Lars seemed relaxed, and, somehow, she sensed he was being genuine, if megalomaniac. But she needed time to unravel all the threads. Time to work out what he was really after. Time she didn't have.

"Come," he said, turning away from the view. "There is something else you have to see."

Leaving the twinkling skyline behind, Mara followed Lars back into the palatial apartment. Violins climbed a trembling scale over the sound system. The glass wall slid shut behind them and the warm air inside was a relief.

"You are my unwilling protégé," said Lars. "So few of my subordinates have your creativity or drive. Their thoughts are consumed by brown-nosing and schemes to get ahead at the expense of their colleagues. They waste their lives playing zero-sum games against each other. But not you. A few years ago you were nothing but a mediocre student at a mid-tier university. On Thursday, you'll be cofounder and CEO of the most coveted new technology company in America. A perfect example of why I love this country so much."

Mara bit back a response. She was Lars's nemesis, not his apprentice. But if he saw her as the latter, perhaps it would streamline her work as the former.

Lars reached out a hand and ran his fingertips along the smooth white wall as he led Mara through a hallway. "Many of my lieutenants would kill for the opportunity and resources I've already afforded you. But they lack the vision to color outside the lines. Their projects are so... banal, so uninspiring. But Mozaik has opened my eyes to the scale at which we can play this game." His smile didn't reach his eyes. "You have a long and lucrative career ahead of you, Ms. Winkel. You're already operating at a level that few ever reach. This is a partnership that will truly make a 'dent in the universe.'"

"I'm happy to hear you're pleased with Mozaik's performance."

"Ah, passive aggression. The last refuge of the damned."

They had traversed the entire floor and stopped in front of a closed set of double doors off the central hallway. Lars put one hand on each door and then paused, looking over his shoulder at Mara.

"Keep that anger burning, Mara," he said. "It is a source of energy even in the darkest of times. But sadly, moxie is not the only quality necessary for you to cultivate as a leader in this venture. You've done a lot right with Mozaik, even if you were trying to thwart me in the process. But there is an essential space in which you are consistently underperforming. As a board member and mentor, it is my duty to help you grow and improve as a manager."

He waited for her to respond. Who did Lars think he was? Darth Vader playing at Yoda? He sounded like The Godfather writing a business self-help book. It would almost be funny if she weren't so damn scared.

"So," she said after a moment. She didn't like this one bit. "Where are we so deficient? I can't wait for your pearl of wisdom." As if she would ever take advice from someone like him.

"It's not enough to be innovative," he said. "You must have *discipline.*"

Lars thrust both arms forward and the double doors flew open.

30

BEYOND THE DOORS was a large sunken living room. The center was covered in thick white shag carpet, and lay two steps below the floor of the rest of the house. Pillows lined the edges, giving the whole space a modernist Roman feel. François and three other men looked up as Lars flung the doors open.

Mara froze. In front of the men, two naked bodies were strapped to chairs with plastic zip ties. One man and one woman. Duct tape covered their mouths and their heads hung down against their chests. Vicious burn marks covered their pale skin.

Mara was transfixed by the smallest of details. The small mole above the woman's navel, the glint of an engagement ring, and the V-neck tan line nestled between her exposed breasts. The lavender bruise blooming on the man's torso, and his flaccid penis peeking out from a nest of bristly black pubic hair.

The man's head rose slowly. He had to shake the hair out of his face. His dark eyes met hers, and only then did she recognize him. Mara's heart stopped. It was James.

The second he realized who she was, James started thrashing in his chair. She could hear him through the duct tape over his mouth. François reached out and a sparking arc of electricity leapt from the taser in his hand to inscribe another burn across James's chest. His body jerked and spasmed.

The woman threw back her head and sweaty strands of curly brown hair flew aside to reveal Danielle's face, one eye indigo and swollen. She surged against the zip ties but the man next to François twisted her nipple violently and backhanded her across the face. She sagged against the bonds and blood dribbled from her ravaged breast.

Time slowed, milliseconds swelling and distending. Ringing filled Mara's ears. This had to be a dream, a nightmare forged of stress and jet lag. James was supposed to be at the hotel. Danielle should be back in Boulder, working with Chad to lead the technical team in James's absence. This couldn't be happening. Not here. Not now. Had Lars laced her brandy with something?

Her thoughts cascaded in irrational patterns, the facts refusing to fit the horror of the scene in front of her. Invisible spider webs held her still. Claustrophobic pressure kept a scream bottled up inside her. It was just like her dreams of the picnic in Pasadena. Primary colors, the smell of barbeque, and then the shots and blood spattering over plates of corn, ribs, and potato chips. James's uncle gunned down by the vestiges of the Taiwanese mafia, from whom his family had fled all the way to California.

The men were all staring right at her, ignoring James and Danielle. Focus. She had to *focus*. She wasn't a deer in the headlights, or a helpless child. Even if this was a goddamn nightmare, she wouldn't let her subconscious get away with it.

Her gun. She was armed for fuck's sake. Her arm seemed to move in slow motion, as if the air was honey. Flicking aside her wool coat, she thrust her hand into the small of her back to draw the pistol from its holster. At the same time, she dropped to one knee on the threshold.

But as she ripped the gun free, an iron grip locked onto her arm. Rough fingers felt for a pressure point and blinding pain erupted up the right side of her body. Through the ringing, she heard the pistol clatter to the floor. Then the hands yanked her arm up behind her back, threatening to dislocate her shoulder. She struggled up from her half-kneeling position and was forced down into the sunken room, the thick shag carpet soft beneath her feet.

Lars had moved to stand beside François, and was murmuring something to him. One of the other men must have moved around beside her while she was trying to take in the situation. She smelled garlic on the hot breath next to her ear.

Lars raised his head and smiled. The expression was neutral and his eyes were flat.

"As I was saying, you lack discipline." His tone hadn't change in the slightest. It was as if he was simply continuing their previous conversation without missing a beat. "Discipline is creativity's twin, the flip side of the same coin." He flicked his thumb to toss an imaginary quarter. "If they aren't in balance, your organization suffers. You'll never reach the level of success you desire. You'll never make a lasting impact. But if discipline and creativity are in perfect concert," he clapped his hands together and his eyes shone, "then the world is yours. Nothing can stand in your way and your legacy is assured, inevitable."

Mara coughed and spat on the rug. Adrenaline coursed through her veins, trying to find an outlet. "Who are you? An evil twin of Warren Buffett? What are you doing to my friends? What the fuck do you want from me?"

Lars cocked his head to the side. "But I've already answered that question. I'm here to teach you a lesson, Mara. This is a coachable moment, a tipping point, an opportunity for you to pivot your leadership style."

He grabbed a fistful of James's hair and jerked his head up. Then Lars held out his other hand and François deposited a small vial into it. He waved it back and forth under James's nose. James's eyes snapped open and he tried to twitch away from the vial. Lars pocketed it.

"It all started with this little Wunderkind, didn't it?" he said. James's eyes were glazed with fear. "University wasn't challenging enough so he wrote a genius piece of code. You two decided to run with it and start a company. All the cool kids are doing it these days. But then, like so many stupid children, you stuck your noses where they didn't belong. You hacked into the Center for Mathematics and Society and stole their data, Maelstrom's data, my data." Lars shook his head. "Of course you didn't realize what you had. But we knew." He looked up at Mara. "It was especially obvious after your pathetic little boyfriend tried to play detective. He got what was coming to him, of course, but it can be so frustrating to watch promising young people throw their lives away."

Mara wrenched her arm, trying to drive her shoulder back into the man holding her. But it was about as effective as wrestling a locomotive. "Wriggly little fish," he said. She smelled garlic again and a wave of nausea rose inside her.

"Then you tried to double cross me during the DVG implementation," said Lars. "But you were so easy to manipulate, it was almost no fun at all." He shook his head sadly. "Though the payoff was well worth the disappointment. Seeing the look on Wallis's face... His absence left a vacuum my plans could finally fill. And with the stakes that much higher, it was time to end our little game of cat and mouse. That is why I made the consequences of disobedience explicit. Any successful partnership requires open and direct lines of communication, no?" His eyebrows lifted with the inflection of his voice.

If muscle wasn't going to get her out of this, she'd have to think her way through. Why was Lars doing this? What did he want from them? She could hear James and Danielle breathing shallowly through their noses.

"Everything James and Danielle have done, they did on my orders," said Mara, quietly. "There's no need to do this to them."

"Ah, well," said Lars, the corners of his lips turning down. "That is simply incorrect. Did I say anything about rebellion? If you had betrayed me directly, this evening would have gone very differently. But that's not what this is about. This is about *discipline*." The last word was as sharp as a chef's knife.

Lars moved between James and Danielle, and placed a hand on each of their bare shoulders. James twitched, but couldn't get away. Danielle didn't react, her head hung against her chest. Mara struggled again, but got nowhere.

"True leaders control their ranks," said Lars. "They keep tabs on their team and take part in all critical decisions. But the minute their subordinates step out of line, the leader's power starts to slip. That slippage frays their organization like tearing a scrap of cotton. Thread by thread, their efforts unravel. New revelations come to light at just the wrong times. Competitors take advantage of the disarray to start invading new territory. Vultures circle overhead, waiting for the carrion feast. That is how leaders fall." James grunted behind the duct tape. Lars's grip had tightened, his fingers digging into their shoulders. Lars released them, and left red marks on their flesh.

Lars closed his eyes. Then snapped them open, staring straight at Mara.

"I am helping you more than you know," he said. "When I spot someone with ambition, with talent, I must push them to become the best they can be. It is a weakness of mine." He turned both of his hands palm up in front of his chest, and extended one to James and one to Danielle. "While you were on your road show, these two were fomenting a plan. Their antics threaten this entire bet. Threaten Mozaik. Threaten our partnership."

Mara's thoughts were racing as fast as her heart. What the hell was he talking about? James and Danielle had been safely back in Boulder preparing Mozaik for the massive scaling that the IPO, and subsequent acquisitions would precipitate. She had been the one beginning to foment a scheme, starting to lay the groundwork for a long-term strike against Maelstrom. But she hadn't yet had the opportunity to fill in James on her planning, on how they couldn't simply rely on Xavier and CyFi to get the job done for them. Was this some colossal mix up? Had Lars somehow caught wind of her efforts, and thought that James was behind them? No. She had done nothing incriminating. Nothing overt. And there was nothing to trace back to James because he didn't even know about it yet. So what the fuck has sparked this nightmare scenario?

Lars was still standing there staring at her. "Discipline is unpleasant, those that revel in it face the same fate as narcissists and sadists. But discipline is necessary. Without it, you walk willingly to the chopping block. It is a hard lesson to learn, especially in a country that coddles its citizens like this one. And that brings us all to the present moment, to where we stand today."

He waggled the open palm next to James. "He should be punished for endangering the play. But we cannot afford to have the CTO of Mozaik disappear for its inaugural moment on the grand stage of global commerce. Institutional investors abhor uncertainty and the management team of any company going through an IPO must survive intact, or face the wrath of a bidding rout on opening day. We have too much at stake, on paper and in reputation, to allow such a failure. It would slow our growth, and embarrass too many friends. A pity, but sometimes people really are saved by the bell."

He waggled the palm next to Danielle. "But the accomplice? She has no such deus ex machina waiting in the wings. The market won't mourn her loss and her disobedience demands retribution. What is the maxim again? Ah, yes. Hire slow, fire fast. In this case, discipline requires more than firing. Here in North America, the days of public hangings are over. We won't be able to make it a spectacle, but intimacy has its own emotional appeal, for those lucky enough to present."

A terrible sense of inevitability rose inside of Mara. It invaded every cell, every pore, every breath. She didn't want to see where this was going. She didn't want any more blood on her hands. She didn't want a source of new nightmares. Someone had to find them. Someone had to rescue them. A scream welled up from inside her. It started deep in her abdomen, gained momentum in her chest, and exploded from her mouth.

The rough hand of the man holding her fumbled to block her mouth and cut off the scream. She bit his finger and tasted copper. He swore and jerked the hand away. But a moment later it was back, holding a piece of cloth over her mouth and she couldn't produce more than muffled grunts.

"Mara," said Lars. "Focus. This is important. Disobedience is a cancer. You must excise it. When there are whispers, you must silence them. And when there is an oversight of this magnitude, you must cull it."

The open palm in front of Danielle snapped into a fist. The man standing behind her reached forward and grabbed each side of her head in a meaty hand. His fingers tightened, locking into her tangled hair. He pulled her head up and her good eye blinked slowly, trying to fight through the haze of shock and pain. Mara tried to bite, scream, anything, but her captor held firm. James was moaning and rocking side to side in his chair, which didn't budge.

And then the man twisted Danielle's neck in a fluid motion that produced a sickening, wet cracking sound. He released his hands and stepped back. Now all Mara could see was the back of Danielle's head, turned 180 degrees like an owl's, and canted off to the side at an unnatural angle. Her naked body thrashed against the zip ties, muscles twitching as if in seizure.

With every ounce of being, Mara wanted to look away. She wanted to disappear. To teleport to somewhere safe where they could all laugh this off over a beer. But Danielle's wind-up toy movements held the room's attention in a gravitational pull. No matter what Mara did, her eyes remained glued to the way Danielle's chestnut hair fell onto her bleeding chest. How her hands clutched at themselves, each digit uncoordinated.

The only thing more horrific than the flailing was the stillness that followed. It was a delicate, inviolable thing. They were becalmed in the eye of the storm.

"That," said Lars, his voice hardly above a whisper and his stare boring into Mara, "is discipline."

31

FRANÇOIS DROPPED Mara and James off at their hotel, with the promise that Danielle would be found a few days later, the victim of a tragic car accident on Interstate 225 in Denver. In the meantime, everything would continue as planned. Lars had sent along a bottle of Armagnac with a handwritten note, "To a long and fruitful partnership."

Mara had to try four times before she successfully inserted the key into the lock. They both stumbled into her hotel room. She turned and slid the chain into place with trembling hands. As if a door chain would do anything to stop these people.

Then she went into the bathroom and poured the brandy down the drain, watching as the amber liquid swirled and eddied around the sink. Looking up, she saw a stranger in the mirror staring back at her. The fluorescent lighting ruthlessly illuminated haunted eyes in a face slack with shock. It mesmerized her for a moment. Then she shook her head and looked away, remembering the time she had drowned in the strangeness of her reflection, after trying mushrooms for the first time in high school. If only this were nothing more than a bad trip.

Tossing the empty bottle into the trash, she dug her hand back into her purse, and felt around with her fingers. There. She fished out her phone, unlocked it, and ended the audio recording app she had turned on prior to setting out to meet Lars earlier this afternoon. Four hours and seventeen minutes of audio. She still couldn't believe they hadn't confiscated her phone. They had been worried about their phones being hijacked for so long, she realized she might be able to use the damn thing to her advantage. Hubris. The weakness of a megalomaniac. Lars must be so confident in his command of the situation that details like this could slip through the cracks. They hadn't even taken away her gun, until she tried to use it.

Removing the battery and replacing both pieces in her purse, she reemerged into the hotel room. The freshly pressed sheets, muted colors, and tasteful decorations made her feel like a refugee in a land of corporate normalcy.

James sat on the end of the bed, hands clasped in his lap. Except for the fact that he was staring at a blank television screen, he looked oddly calm. They had given him back his clothes, and his Star Wars shirt looked no more rumpled than during the meeting this afternoon. François and his goons had been careful. All the bruises of taser burns were on his torso. To all outward appearances, James could have been lounging around at the hotel all evening.

Mara sat down next to him, and wrapped an arm around his shoulders. She could feel the tension knotted there, belying his apparent tranquility. It transported her back to their conversation on the bridge over Boulder Creek. Sunshine sparkling on swirling currents that carried dead leaves careening downstream. *The only way out is forward.* That's what she had told James. How hollow those words sounded now.

He turned his head and looked straight into her eyes. Their faces were inches apart, and his gaze was a black hole. She tightened her lips, trying to keep from breaking down.

"I killed her," he said, voice steady. "I killed my fiancé."

Mara slapped him full across the face. A red spot bloomed on his cheek. He touched it with his fingertips and then examined them, disbelieving.

"Don't you *dare* say that," her voice was a snarl. "Not now, not ever. This was not your fault. Nobody takes responsibility for this except for Lars and Maelstrom."

"But I put her at risk, I put us all at risk," said James, clasping his hands and replacing them in his lap. "If we hadn't patched the bug, none of this would have happened."

"James, remember what you told me that night on the roof of your building?" The night a clandestine kiss derailed their friendship for almost a year. "You told me that Craig's murder wasn't my fault even though I had been blaming myself since it happened. Yes, we've all made mistakes. We've all done things that have consequences we couldn't imagine. But that does not make you culpable for cold-blooded murder. That's bullshit. You're too damn smart for that."

They sat in silence for what felt like a long time, the mattress compressing beneath them to press their bodies against each other. The heating system kicked on with a low hum. The little green light glowed on her laptop charger over on the desk. Laughs filtered in from the hallway, a happy couple returning to their room.

Somehow, talking to James was reeling her back in from the abyss of shock at what had just happened. His fiancé had just been murdered in front of them by the man that had been manipulating them for years. He needed something solid to hold on to. She was a poor option given the state she was in herself, but at the moment she was the only option. They were fellow refugees holed up in this posh New York City hotel. It made her wonder how real the veneer of civilization actually was. Violence was swimming just beneath the surface, always ready to rear its ugly head.

"What are we going to do, Mara?" James asked in a small voice.

"Let's start at the beginning," she said quietly. "Why did you tell me you were drinking coffee on that conference call?"

32

JAMES TOOK A NUMBER OF SLOW BREATHS. He relaxed the muscles in his shoulders with visible effort. His bangs hung down over his eyes, greasy with cold sweat. Mara bit the inside of her cheek, not sure what to expect.

"She discovered it," said James. "Danielle, she found the needle in the haystack. Originally we thought it was a bug. But it turned out to be much more than that."

"What exactly are you talking about?" Mara said gently, prodding not pushing.

"It never made sense, how they forced Chad on us at the last minute," said James.

"Wait, Chad Zhukov?"

"Yeah. What with the road show and everything. We had so much preparation to do. I mean, everything else helped us move faster. Leslie, Zach. They all have skillsets that we don't have on our team, yet. We aren't investment bankers or corporate lawyers. Grant, too. Gordon didn't know how to tighten us up for an IPO and anyway, he's happier as Head of Accounting than he ever was as CFO. We might not have chosen the same people ourselves, but by handing us that team, Lars accelerated everything. It would have taken us five times as long to get ready for the day after tomorrow without them."

James coughed and winced. Mara could only imagine how much that hurt his bruised ribs.

"But Chad was different," said Mara. She remembered arguing with James and Vernon about it a month ago, right after Lars had ordered them to install Chad. *Danielle is our VP of Engineering. She's running three teams and four simultaneous implementations right now. We don't need this guy. It's going to hurt us, not help us.*

"Right," said James. "Our engineering process was far from perfect, but we were getting things done and working out the kinks. Bringing in a new VP of Engineering who knows nothing about our product and has never worked with any of our people is just crazy, especially when we were gearing up to deploy at scale. It would slow us down just as the IPO help was speeding us up."

Mara thought back to when Chad had arrived. It had been a few weeks before the start of the road show. She had been focused on getting ready for the IPO, while James was managing the product team.

"But Chad seemed up to speed pretty quickly," she said. She didn't remember any major issues coming up, despite how much she had dreaded hiring him.

"That's what made me more suspicious," said James. "The day he arrived, he knew more about our algorithms than many of our own engineers. He got oriented faster than anyone I've ever worked with. It was almost as if he had been through the code before. And now it's obvious. He'd been over *every line* of our code before."

"What?" said Mara. "What the fuck? How is that possible?" Any leak of their source code was a major breach of security. That code defined Mozaik's value. If it were to be released into the wild, they wouldn't have a proprietary service to offer at all. Anybody could build off of it and do whatever they wanted with it. It would undermine their entire business.

James shrugged. "I have no idea," he said. "I assume Lars must have somehow gotten him a copy."

"But—"

James waved a hand. "Don't worry, that's not the important part. The important part is what Danielle discovered the day after you flew to L.A. for the first set of pitches."

"Go on, then," said Mara. "What did she find?" Her head was spinning. There were just too many data to keep track of, too many balls in the air. What was the central theme tying them all together? What infernal scheme skulked at the center of this madness?

"At first, we thought it was just a bug," said James. "We hadn't seen it anywhere before, and didn't take it too seriously. We tracked it and then started working on a patch. But the harder we tried to fix it, the more intentional it looked."

"Someone inserted a bug into our code on purpose."

"Not just any bug," said James. "A back door. After a marathon session messing around with it, we figured out that it did two things. First, it gave root level access to anyone with the right key that knew how to exploit it."

Another piece of Mara's world sloughed away, like a berg off an ice shelf. Anyone with root level access could do absolutely anything they wanted with Mozaik. Crash it. Subvert it. Reengineer it.

"What else did it do?" she asked.

"Second, it inserted a tracking module into Mozaik. As we map a financial data set, it sorted accounts with a unique tag in their metadata into a special bin. The accounts in that special bin never go through our analysis engine, but automatically get reported as clean. It's a classic man-in-the-middle attack. The client, and even our internal administrators, would never see a difference on their dashboards. Mozaik would map and analyze a data set and spit out the results and nobody would be the wiser that a small fraction of that data got a false positive."

"Fucking A," said Mara. "It's a get-out-of-jail-free card."

James nodded. "Exactly. Any account holding the card gets a pass."

"But that's a serious set of protocols," said Mara. "This isn't some shoddy workaround. Wouldn't that kind of thing take time to build?"

"Hell yeah," said James. "It was pretty clean too, from a technical perspective. This wasn't a slash and burn job, it was highly sophisticated."

"And it puts everything at risk," said Mara. She was glad to be sitting on the bed. She didn't think her legs could handle standing right now.

"It sabotages Mozaik," said James. "There's no other way to say it. So, Danielle and I tried to fix it. There's no way we could scale up with that kind of hole, and the last thing we wanted was for this to blow up right as we're going public. So we hacked a quick patch together, to close the back door. Then, we tried to undo the get-out-of-jail-free card. But immediately after we pushed out the release with the patch, Chad stormed into my office, and demanded I reverse it."

James shook his head. "I refused, obviously, citing the problems the patch solved. But he just responded that if I didn't reverse the patch, and leave that bit of code as it was, that there would be consequences." He hunched his upper body. "I told him I was his boss, and that he could pack up his desk right now and leave the building. He just laughed, and told me to go fuck myself. That was two days ago."

He shivered next to her, and Mara gave him another squeeze. "And you were trying to signal to me that something was wrong on the conference call. Obviously you couldn't talk about it in front of the group and you were worried about being recorded over the phone, so you had to wait to tell me until we saw each other today in New York. But I couldn't find you after the meeting this afternoon."

James hugged himself and nodded. "A guy came in right as the meeting ended and said they had a call waiting for me in another room. I walked through the door and then everything just went black." Air hissed between his teeth. "I woke up on that chair on the white carpet. Danielle was tied up next to me." He coughed again, the sound wet and rasping. "They kept asking us questions, and then hitting or tasering us when we didn't respond fast enough. But I don't think they were really interested in our answers. They were just killing time, until you and Lars arrived. And then..."

James stood up and the memory foam mattress oozed back into shape. He took two small steps forward and gripped the edges of the widescreen TV, mounted on the wall. Mara thought that he was going to tear it down and smash it. But he just pressed his forehead against the cool glass. He stood there for a minute, and Mara wasn't sure what to do. About this or anything. Every time she thought she had put out a fire, another one turned out to be blazing right behind her. There was no end to the machinations put in place to ruin them and Mozaik. Cluster fuck didn't even begin to cover it.

Then James turned back to her, favoring his side. "She's dead, Mara. She's *dead*." A sob wracked his body as if he had been fighting as hard as he could to keep it in check.

She stood and wrapped him up in a tight bear hug. "I know," she said, "I know." And then she was crying too. Another body to add to her karmic tab. Another life snuffed out to further the plans of a madman.

She wished she could tell James that it would all be okay, that everything would somehow turn out all right. But Craig was still an ache that seemed to have no reprieve. Quinn still visited her in dreams. And Maria. Mara thought of all the bouquets abandoned anonymously on her doorstep. The void in her expression at the funeral could have turned a person to stone.

Bereavement wasn't something to recover from. It was something to endure. Sometimes absence had more weight than reality. It wouldn't be okay. It wouldn't turn out all right. Danielle was gone, and her ghost would haunt them for the rest of their lives. James's shaking body felt like a young boy's in her arms, skinny under the big Star Wars t-shirt. *A New Hope.* That was exactly what they needed. That was exactly what she needed to find them.

33

SLEEP WAS OUT OF THE QUESTION. While James took a hot shower in his room, Mara called the front desk and reserved one of the hotel's conference rooms. Then she grabbed the pad of stationery from the desk and made a list, outlining a check box next to each item. It was time to go over and pick up James.

He had pulled on jeans and a t-shirt featuring the alt/option key from a Mac keyboard. His face looked drawn and his eyes were hollow. But at least the steam had scoured away the snot and tears and refreshed his tangled black hair. Scooping up their laptops and phones, they took the elevator down to the conference room.

It was a large room with a large table in the middle and a few seating alcoves clustered along the walls. The wide windows looked out on a bustling New York City night. Mara checked the time, 11 p.m., Boulder would have been quiet. But here, pedestrians and cars muscled through the streets with the urgency of rush hour. Neon signs flickered and windows glowed up and down the surrounding skyscrapers.

They colonized one end of the conference table and Mara called for a concierge. He arrived a few minutes later. She pulled the list from her pocket and unfolded it.

"I would very much appreciate it, if you could help us acquire these items," she said. His eyes widened as he read over the list. She pulled out five hundred dollars in cash and pressed it into his hand. "Are you the night shift?"

"Yes, ma'am," he said, accepting the wad. "I get off at 8 a.m."

"Great," said Mara. "We will likely need more of your help this evening but that should get us started. We also very much appreciate your discretion."

He tipped his hat and grinned. "You got it. Anything you need, just let me know."

After he had hustled out the door, James frowned. "What was that about?"

"Basic stuff," said Mara. "He should be back soon. You got your phone?"

"Yeah, of course."

"Great, here." She handed him another pad of stationery. "Copy out the contacts for your family and the most important people at Mozaik."

"Why?"

"You'll see, just do it."

They both sat in silence for a few minutes, scribbling out their key contact numbers and email addresses. Then Mara turned off and disassembled her phone. James followed suit.

"Just a precaution," she said.

"Why do we need precautions?" he asked, eyes narrowed. "We're at Lars's mercy. We just need to put our heads down and do what he says. Otherwise we just put more people at risk."

Mara's fingers drummed on the table. James was right. She remembered how the green smoothie had spilled all over Lars's shirt when he handed her the envelope of surveillance photos in the back of the SUV. She thought of her parents, who were flying in separately from California the next day to attend the IPO festivities. Anything they did to oppose Maelstrom endangered their loved ones. Lars had demonstrated again and again that his threats were anything but empty.

On the other hand, cooperating with Lars was no guarantee of immunity. The deeper they dug into his schemes, the more of a potential liability they became. The only clean break possible would involve fatality. They were trapped. He could promise power and riches all he liked, but a posh cell was still a cell.

They had designed Mozaik from day one to combat organized crime, not abet it. If they launched Mozaik with the changes Chad had implemented, their software would become Maelstrom's operating system for fraud, and they would be as guilty as Lars. That's how these games worked. You found leverage over people, and then turned them into your pawns. And she was sick of being a pawn.

"Remember when David told us about pivots?" asked Mara.

"Sure," said James. "Making a major shift to business strategy because your current model isn't working."

"Right, that's why we shifted from serving individual accountants to working with banks," said Mara. "I think it's time for another pivot. We tried attacking Lars by running an analysis against him at DVG. We tried working with Xavier and CyFi to bring him down as part of a long-term investigative strategy. We tried reactively fixing the hatchet job he's making of Mozaik. None of those are working. We need to do something way outside-the-box. Something so radical he won't expect it. That's the only way we're going to sneak through his contingency planning."

"But he'll kill us," said James. "He'll kill our families."

"Do you really think they'll be safe even if we cooperate?" asked Mara. "You have more experience with this than I do. What would the Taiwanese mafia do?"

James was silent. Then he swiped the hair from in front of his eyes. "No, you're right. They own us. Sooner or later they'll push too hard, and people will get hurt. Slaves never have the right to object."

He took a shuddering breath. "But Mara, I can't let anyone else die because of me. I just can't."

"Me neither," said Mara, her stomach turning. "Which is why I think we need to act fast."

"What are you talking about?"

A knock on the door made them both jump. Mara stood to open it. The concierge entered carrying two big bags. He unpacked their contents on the table. Two large to-go cups. A small whiteboard with a tripod and set of colored pens. A case of energy drinks. One steaming pizza piled with toppings. A roll of paper towels. An elegant box containing a complete set of the ancient strategy board game, *go*. Five prepaid smart phones. An extra large bag of gummy bears and a pack of dark chocolate covered almonds.

"Thank you," said Mara. "We'll need another double cap extra dry and oolong tea every hour, on the hour."

The concierge mock saluted and hurried off.

James removed the plastic lid and peered into his cup, steam wafting up over his face.

"Supplies?" he asked.

"That's right," she said. "Neither of us will be able to sleep tonight anyway."

"Why *go*?"

"Because I'm sick of letting Lars choose the game."

34

HOT MOZZARELLA BURNED THE ROOF of Mara's mouth as she took a bite of pizza. She hadn't noticed until now, but she was hungry. Neither of them had eaten anything since lunch. James had just stared at his piece but started to eat when she prodded him. Then they both gobbled down two slices each before taking so much as a breath.

Hunger sated, Mara sat back and wiped her mouth with a paper towel. "You weren't the only one with secrets to share," she said. "There are a number of things that I'm overdue to catch you up on."

"Alright," he said, frowning. "What's going on?"

"Senator Hartfer sponsored the American STEM Education Act," she said.

"Are you kidding me?"

"Nope, he led the bill through Congress."

"What about Juliana?"

"It was her idea and she did everything she could to get it passed," said Mara. "But she works for the President and has no official sway on the Hill. Hartfer is the one who pushed it over the hump."

Something tugged at the edge of her thinking. It had been freezing while they were admiring the view from Lars's balcony. *That's why I had Donald pass the STEM Act.* "Shit! That reminds me."

Mara opened her laptop, connected to the hotel's wifi, and

ran a search. James cracked his knuckles impatiently. There it was. Senator Donald G. Hartfer. *The banks have been begging the White House for concrete financial security guidelines for years. That law makes Mozaik the gold star that absolves them from liability. No banking executive on Earth can afford not to implement your software.* Lars had openly admitted to ordering Hartfer to pass the bill.

She looked up and James raised his eyebrows. "You said that Chad's back door would have taken an expert significant time to build, right?"

"Yeah," said James. "It had obviously been in the works for a long time."

It was on the tip of her mental tongue. A stray thought just out of reach. *And you, Mara Winkel, have a very important part to play in this little coup. Mozaik is my Trojan Horse.* There was so much going on, so many disparate threads. But a common pattern was emerging from the madness.

"Will you stop that? It's driving me nuts."

"Huh?" She shook her head. "What?"

James reached over and pressed a hand to her knee. It had been tapping incessantly against the bottom of the table.

"Sorry, just thinking," she said.

"Me too," he said. "But that's not helping."

She remembered Xavier's burn scars, how she had ambushed him with a pan of boiling olive oil, after discovering the gun in her apartment. How had he described Maelstrom? *They run the largest money-laundering cartel on Earth. We refer to them as Maelstrom, just like their venture fund with the same name. Their network of shell companies and relationships around the world is enormous. They are the financiers behind many drug and human trafficking rings, illegal arms dealers, and organized crime outfits.* After their last jog, Xavier had added that Mozaik going public must benefit Lars in some larger way. The pieces were falling into place.

Lars had seen potential in Mozaik after reviewing how James hacked the Center for Mathematics and Society, one of Maelstrom's many money laundries. Once he saw what they could do, he had invested in them for strategic reasons, just like so many legitimate corporate venture funds did all the time. Except his plans weren't hampered by legality or ethics. He manipulated them into ousting his rival within Maelstrom during the DVG sting.

But that was nothing compared to his long-term vision. Senator Hartfer was already in his pocket so he ordered him to ensure the success of Juliana's initiative. The American STEM Education Act guaranteed Mozaik's deployment in all major global banking institutions. That guarantee meant they would have to go public to finance the extraordinary growth required to service demand. That's why they needed to buy AMQ, Larsons, and Udemas. By rolling those up, Mozaik would instantly become one of the most important financial services firms on Earth. But he wouldn't even have to finance it himself, investors would pile on to participate in an opportunity like this. So, Lars deployed his IPO dream team to speed them through the process. The IPO had the added bonus of legitimizing Mozaik in the eyes of Wall Street and Washington, reducing the potential for blowback.

Meanwhile, he had Chad Zhukov working on a hack to turn Mozaik into a literal Trojan. No need for phishing or anything so unsophisticated. Lars simply installed Chad as Head of Engineering so that he could build it directly into the source code. Mozaik's software was already running in a number of large banks and preapproved to deploy in hundreds more as soon as they could service them. Lars would have a direct backdoor into the entire international financial system. Even better, Mozaik's algorithms would systematically root out and destroy the fraud schemes of his criminal rivals, while leaving Maelstrom's accounts untouched. The STEM Act guaranteed a monopoly for Mozaik. In turn, Mozaik guaranteed a criminal monopoly for Maelstrom.

It was beautiful, in a fucked-up kind of way. One big goddamn circle jerk. Win. Win. Win. That's why Lars treated her like a protégé, offering Armagnac in one hand and death in the other. *This is the stick.* That was the caption on the photo of Derrick's mangled body right after they raised their seed round. That's all it ever was with Lars, carrots and sticks. Craig. Derrick. Quinn. Danielle. Each of them had threatened to gum up the works, picking at the edges of Lars's big idea.

And so he had swatted each of them away like flies, ordering their deaths, without a second thought. Quinn had quit Denver PD because the new Commissioner had sidelined the investigation into Craig's murder. *It's a fucking disgrace but nobody can do anything about it because he's so connected with Senator Hartfer.* When you bought off people at the top, everything else was easy. Their fingers must extend even to CyFi, shutting down the probe into a Hartfer connection. Just the cost of doing business.

But these were the very, very few that she was aware of. She could only imagine how long the list of Lars's victims must run. The managers of international cartels didn't have time for the friction of conscience. It was merely a matter of efficiency and risk management after all. And their clients were *very* demanding.

"Mara," said James, his voice dead calm. "It's all been one big gambit. He's been playing us from the very beginning."

She returned from her reverie and could see in his eyes that James was thinking the same thing she was. A lump rose in her throat and she reached out and grabbed her best friend's hand. She was standing barefoot in the grass. James's uncle Chiu was bleeding out on the Pasadena picnic table. James had been ten years old. While everyone else just stood there like deer in the headlights, he had grabbed his mom's phone and dialed 911.

Others might be awed by his genius, but Mara loved James for his tranquility in the face of adversity. She raged against the storm while he rose above it. It was what made them such a good team.

"I don't know about you," she said. "But I'm tired of this pawn shit."

There was a knock on the door.

"Ms. Winkel, you said every hour on the hour. One oolong, one double cap extra dry." The concierge entered and deposited two more steaming paper cups on the table, clearing away the empty ones. "You two working on a big business deal or something?"

"A little of both," said Mara. "And thanks for the drinks, keep 'em coming."

35

"WE SHOULD TAKE THIS TO XAVIER," said James, leaning in over the table. "CyFi should know what to do in these kinds of situations."

Mara's heart sank. They had been so focused leading up to the IPO that she hadn't set aside time to bring James up to date on this. It was important but not urgent. Today had changed everything. "About that," she said. "I don't think CyFi is an option anymore."

"What? Why?"

Mara could almost hear the Lebanese pop music that played during her last meal with Juliana. *In my experience, the best way to fix the system is not to trust it in the first place.* "After realizing that Senator Hartfer had sponsored the bill, I asked Xavier what CyFi had found out about his connection to Lars. He was meeting with Lars and Dominic when Craig was murdered, I was there. Obviously, I told Xavier right after it happened, and he promised that CyFi would follow up. Well, turns out they didn't. Someone high up apparently shut off pursuit of that lead before it had even gotten started. Above Xavier's 'pay grade.'" She spat out the last word.

"So you think CyFi is in on the whole thing," said James, sipping his tea.

"Not as such," said Mara. The burn marks were so red and puffy on Xavier's skin. It made her cringe to think of them. Their fling, if that was the word for it, had been a pleasant diversion. A no-strings-attached affair had been exactly what she needed, especially with one of the few people on Earth she could actually talk to about this insane house of cards.

"I think Xavier and their field agents are doing their best." She shrugged. "But there's definitely something compromising CyFi from the top down. Quinn told me ages ago that Hartfer pulled the strings to get the new Denver Police Commissioner appointed, the guy who mothballed the investigation into Craig's death. I wouldn't be surprised if it was the same culprit here. Hartfer's on the Senate Intelligence Committee. He must know about CyFi. No doubt he's got influence there, too."

She shook her head and took a sip of cappuccino. The earthy acidity was an odd way to wash down pizza, but not unpleasant. "No," she said. "I want to notify Xavier and his agents only at the last possible moment, before there's time for critical information to filter up the chain of command. Just like Juliana did with her colleagues when we ran the DVG sting. If possible, we want to eliminate them from strategic decision-making and only involve them for tactical operations. Any oversight from them might give our enemies a peep hole."

"Well isn't this more of a mess than ever," said James, knuckles white where he gripped the edge of the table. "We're being forced to launch the biggest black market financial tool in history and we can't go to the cops or even federal intelligence agencies for help."

"Too big to fail," said Mara. "Petty thieves go to jail. But the masterminds behind the Financial Crisis or the hedge funds who developed high frequency trading? They got private islands, or, better yet, appointments at the SEC or the Fed."

"This is why I hate Wall Street," said James. "People play games for money as if they don't even realize it's just a proxy for value. They think money is an end in itself. It's as if athletes just started buying medals off eBay instead of winning them at the Olympics.

Can't they see the bigger picture?"

Mara snorted. She had spent the entire road show in front of people who had devoted their entire lives to playing the markets and acquiring wealth. They were the water that bankers, like Zach, swam in. "It's just a score to tally for them," she said. "It's like racking up goals in foosball. The traders I've met with over the past month value money less than anyone I've ever met. They're not greedy, they're ultra-competitive. They're the douchebag who cheats at a game of poker with friends, just to see if he can. Or pretends to be fouled in basketball so he can take a free throw at a critical point in the game. Take that guy, multiply him by ten thousand, and mix in an Ivy League degree and a long-term cocaine problem. Winning is a dangerous addiction."

"It's just so... lame." James rubbed his chin.

"That's why we're not doing it."

"But where does that leave us? If we can't get help from the government, how in the world can we strike back at Maelstrom? They'll just reach out and crush us."

"Hmm," said Mara, sitting back. "There's one person in government who hates Wall Street as much as you do." She drained the last of her second cappuccino. "Pass me one of those phones."

James slid a burner across the table to her. She powered it up and consulted her list of contacts. It felt funny to have a paper list of names. It was retro, like Oregon Trail or Michael Jackson. Everything before that night felt equally anachronistic, another time, another world.

"Remember when you recorded Dominic's rant when they tried to squeeze us on the seed round?" Despite everything, Mara couldn't keep a grin off her face.

James nodded and leaned back in his chair.

"Well," said Mara, "after the meeting ended this afternoon, Lars asked me to go back to the apartment with him. I told him I needed to go to the bathroom before we left and while I was in the stall, I turned on an audio recording app on my phone."

James stared at her. "They didn't take it away?"

She shook her head. "I couldn't believe it myself. But they didn't even confiscate my gun, until I pulled it from the holster. I think they're so confident in their own strength, they think they're invincible."

"Whoa," said James. Something fluttered behind his eyes. It was like a single out of place shot in a stop motion animation. "You recorded all of it? Even—"

"Yes." Mara cut him off. She had just lost a close friend. But James had lost his fiancé. She wanted to pull him tight so that they could cry on each other's shoulders. She wanted to give him space to wrestle the grief, to orient himself in the emotional wasteland their lives had become. But they lacked even that small luxury. If they were going to do anything, they needed to do it now and do it well. They needed to focus.

Once this was all over, they would have more than enough time for mourning. Or not. One way or the other, an endgame was an endgame. She picked up the burner and dialed.

36

"MA'AM?" A timid voice inquired from behind the closed doors. "I have your drinks, and there's a Ms. Juliana Estevez here to see you."

"Come on in," said Mara, standing up.

The concierge opened the doors, cups in hand. Juliana stepped through behind him. Her severe dark suit and perfect posture made her look like a sculptor had carved her from solid granite. But when she surveyed the room, her stern expression turned bemused.

"Ma'am," asked the concierge. "Can I get you something to drink?"

"Please," said Juliana. "Drip coffee, black."

He nodded and ducked out of the room, pulling the doors closed behind him.

"Hi," said James, raising a hand.

"What *is* this place?" asked Juliana, gesturing to take in the pizzas, *go* set, whiteboard, laptops, and phones scattered across the wide conference table.

"You should see our new Boulder offices," said Mara. "Each conference room has a superhero theme." She thought back to the modest gray scale that had graced Juliana's various offices. They had always smelled so strongly of sage. "We see it as a way to keep our top talent happy. I think you would probably characterize it as a 'gross misuse of funds.'"

Juliana gave a tight-lipped smile. "I probably would. You Silicon

Valley kids just don't know when to stop."

"Please," said Mara. "We're Boulder kids. You know that."

"Eh," Juliana waved a hand as if to dismiss the entire American West. "So, you said on the phone that you were organizing that fishing trip we talked about over falafel."

"And I'm impressed by your response time," Mara said, offering her a slice of pizza. "I didn't think we'd be seeing you until tomorrow at the earliest."

"Anything to get out of another meeting with the Fed," said Juliana. "And midnight rendezvous tend to be far more interesting than midday ones."

Mara had expected to wake her up from her bed in Washington but Juliana had picked up on the first ring. She was on a two-week trip to New York doing reviews of cybersecurity measures at the Federal Reserve, and hating every minute of it. Mara had reached her when she was midway through writing a late-night report in her hotel room on the other side of Manhattan.

"To answer your earlier question," said Mara. "This is a war room of sorts. And the fishing trip is happening way ahead of schedule."

"I gathered as much."

"Your phone is off and disassembled?" asked James, holding up his phone's battery.

Juliana nodded. "I learned that protocol last time I saw Mara in D.C."

"Take a seat and we'll bring you up to speed," said Mara.

Juliana sat and Mara supplied her with a notepad, pen, and burner.

"You said the target was a money laundering cartel larger than the one we took down in the DVG sting, which was the largest bust of its kind in recorded history," said Juliana, narrowing her eyes.

"The U.N. estimates that transnational organized crimes generate about $2 trillion a year in profits or approximately 15-20 percent of global GDP," said James.

"We suspect that Maelstrom has a significant portion of that capital under management," said Mara. "They clean it, invest it, and manage it on behalf of their criminal clientele. They're Wall Street's dark alley, the bad guy bank." Mara ran a hand through her hair. She needed a shower. "And just like lots of other banks out there, they suddenly realized that technology was important and scrambled to get ahead of the curve. That's how they ended up investing in Mozaik in the first place."

Juliana coughed. "What did you just say?" Her incredulity was palpable.

Mara grimaced. "We have a lot to catch you up on."

37

"SO," said Juliana, eyes like drill bits. "You're telling me that the largest anti-money laundering sting in modern history, the sting we executed together, was orchestrated by an even larger cartel called Maelstrom?"

"I'm afraid that's right," said Mara. "Maelstrom was our target the whole time. Lars tricked us into taking out his main rival within the organization and guaranteeing his ascendancy."

"But Lars and his associates were *already* investors in Mozaik? You were working for him?" Juliana's knuckles were white.

"Yes," said Mara. "As I said, he led our seed financing round." Mara had to stop her foot tapping on the floor again. Of course Juliana would react this way. She should have anticipated this. She wasn't a knight in shining armor who could ride in and solve all their problems. Juliana had never known any of Mozaik's history with Lars, or the bloody aftermath of the DVG operation. To her this was all new. It flipped her world upside-down. It was incriminating. It pained Mara to think that she hadn't even considered how this backstory would impact Juliana's own life.

"This is a waste of time," said James, swiping the hair out of his face. "We need to deal with what's happening right now."

Juliana turned to him slowly. "*A waste of time?*"

James flinched as if acid had been thrown on his face.

"A waste of time?" Juliana repeated, thunderstruck. "I risked my career to side with you and take down DVG. The President appointed me based on the success of the sting. The President of the United States of America. I used that authority to hand Mozaik a monopoly with the STEM Act to scale that success."

Juliana stood, walked around the table and stared out of the window at the traffic passing in the night below. She pressed both palms against the glass and her shoulders shuddered as she took in a series of deep breaths.

"But you didn't know," said James.

Juliana lifted her palms from the glass and slammed them back, shaking the full-length window. "That's the nail in the coffin," she said. "Ignorance is even more damning than culpability." Then her tone changed, as if she were talking to herself. "I can't believe I trusted a couple of *children*."

She turned back to the room. "Mr. Chen, Ms. Winkel," she nodded to each of them in turn, "If you'll excuse me, I have a letter of resignation to write."

"No." Mara stood. Shame flooded through her. Of all the lies that this madness had foisted on her, here was one that reached straight into her gut and twisted. Juliana had dedicated her life to catching bad guys. She had the thankless job of investigating white-collar perps who lined black market pockets but didn't get the attention or prison time of their gangster associates. She had put her principles in front of everything else to stick her neck out and bet on Mozaik. It was her determination and fearlessness that had brought McLeay and Morris to justice. Without her, Mozaik would never be where it was today.

If only she could have been honest with Juliana, since day one. If only she could have told her about Lars, Dominic, Craig, Derrick, Quinn, Hartfer, and all the other fucked up shit going down behind the scenes. But that would have endangered even more people, including Juliana. It would have put Mozaik and everything else at risk.

Now it was a moot point anyway. They couldn't very well ask for Juliana's help without telling her what was really going on. But that meant the news dropped like a guillotine, without the context or grace that Mara yearned to give so that she could understand, so that she *would* understand.

Juliana stared at her, frank disbelief all over her face. "What did you just say to me?"

"No," Mara repeated. "Juliana, I'm sorry we had to break it to you like this. I really am. But I didn't call you in here at midnight to catch you up. I called you in here because there's an emergency."

Juliana shook her head and stepped around the table to collect her things. "I'm sorry but this is completely insane."

Mara pointed to the hall. "You can walk out right now," she said. "Go on back to Washington and deliver your letter of resignation to the President, in person. But Danielle was murdered tonight. The financial system you're tasked with policing is about to be sabotaged at a grand scale. Your passion project, the STEM Act, made that possible. Everything you've worked for will be turned to ash, but nobody will be able to do jack shit about it. If you walk out that door, you condemn us. You condemn your life's work."

Mara gestured to James. "We need your help. We need you to transform Mozaik from an accessory to fraud into its antidote. We've been co-opted and blackmailed for so long it's hard to imagine what it feels like to be free. The worst part is that we've got to put on the dog and pony show. Dress nice, act nice, play nice. We're the hottest tech IPO on Wall Street, and instead of drinking champagne and celebrating with our team, a thug just snapped our Chief Architect's neck and we know that Mozaik, the project that's sucked up the last few years of our lives, is about to make Lars the most powerful cartel boss on Earth. Oh, and we can't go to the police because they're as corrupt as anyone else and we can't even go to CyFi because their leadership may be compromised."

Juliana just stood there. Her mouth worked but no words came out.

"Juliana," said Mara. "This has to stop. We are the only people who even know the full extent of what's going on. There's no one else who has the slimmest chance of stopping it. James and I can't do it alone. We need your expertise, your perspective, your contacts, your credibility." She picked up her disassembled phone from the table. "Is the audio recording enough?"

Juliana put her things back onto the table and collapsed into a chair. Her movements were delicate and teetering, like an old woman. "No," she said, her voice barely above a whisper. "Not even close."

38

"BUT LARS ADMITS WHAT HE'S PLANNING and," James took a shuddering breath, "It even recorded them killing Danielle." His expression was a cocktail of confusion, rage, and desperation.

Juliana shook her head. "At best, it's circumstantial. They're sophisticated operators. I'll bet you they already cleaned out the apartment. Lars, and anyone else in their leadership, will have rock solid alibis that confirm they were somewhere else. You have no hard evidence to substantiate what's in the recording. And digital files can be modified so easily that they can't stand alone. Maelstrom's lawyers would eat it for breakfast and your families would likely have to go into witness protection. It would be a disaster. But that's not even the worst part."

Mara rubbed her eyes, feeling deflated. That recording had been the strand of silver lining she was holding to. "If that's not the worst part, what is?"

Juliana shrugged. "How quickly do you think it would take Maelstrom to replace Lars? Even if you were able to succeed, against all odds, Maelstrom would still be as strong as ever. Sure, a guilty man might go to jail. But did putting Morris and McLeay behind bars have a discernible impact on the global money laundering trade? We jabbed them but at the end of the day, their organizations bounced back stronger than ever. Is that really what you want to repeat with Lars?"

"What else do we need?" asked James.

"I have no idea," said Juliana. "You need more evidence. It needs to be incontrovertible. Then you can use the recording to seal the deal. But it won't stand a chance by itself."

Cut off the head and the snake grows a new one. They needed to target not just the man, but the institution. But they couldn't hope to take on an organization like Maelstrom head-to-head. If they were going to do anything, it had to be clever, not brute. Where was their leverage?

"All I know is that right now there are a lot of balls in the air," said Mara. "The STEM Act. The IPO. The back door. More murder and blackmail." She ticked them off on her fingers. "This is a tipping point, everything's in flux. Once it all settles out, Maelstrom will be too entrenched for us to tackle. But right now, the speed and chaos of their success makes them vulnerable. We need to do something to take advantage of the fact that Lars thinks we're cowering in fear and awe in our hotel rooms. We just have to find the right place to hit them."

James unwrapped *go* and picked up a handful of the smooth black and white stones. He stared at them as he turned them over and over in his palm. "We need to set off a cascade failure," he said, his tone thoughtful, almost academic.

"A what?"

"Like when a massive network collapses because of a single faulty router. A single coding error in a routine update took down 40 percent of Gmail worldwide for eighteen minutes in 2012. When you're operating at scale, tiny mistakes can have massive consequences. The Empire should never have built an unprotected exhaust pipe on the Death Star."

"Excuse me?" asked Juliana.

"Don't worry about it," he said. "Star Wars reference. The point is that Maelstrom is big and powerful, with fingers everywhere. How can we turn that into a weakness?" He dropped the stones and they clicked against each other as they scattered across the board.

"We need to turn their assets into liabilities." Mara rubbed her chin. "I think I have an idea."

39

SWEAT POURED DOWN Mara's face as she sprinted up the stairs two at a time. Breaths came in sharp gasps and muscles burned with accumulated lactic acid. It was depressing to think how long it had been since her last true workout. The least she could do was eschew the elevator.

Juliana was right. The recording just wasn't enough. Even if it were, it would have a limited impact anyway. They'd still be up shit creek. With Maelstrom still intact, they wouldn't have accomplished much of anything.

Throwing a hand out to push off the wall, she charged around the sharp corner and up the next flight. The problem with Juliana's thinking was that she didn't take it far enough. Mozaik was fucked. They had been co-opted by a criminal network that was manipulating their system for their own purposes. But just as someone else would replace Lars if he fell, something else would replace Maelstrom if it fell. Mozaik's algorithms automated financial security at scale. The STEM Act made it the global standard. But the very monopoly that made Mozaik an investor wunderkind during the roadshow painted a target on their software.

People robbed banks because that's where the money was. Mozaik's influence made it vulnerable. Whether it was another criminal cartel or lobbyists seeking commercial advantage, any centralized gatekeeper of financial security could be manipulated. Given the size of the stakes, it was fair to say that such a gatekeeper *would* be manipulated. Lars had gotten in first. But even if they could oust him, there would be an endless queue of frauds, schemers, and hedge fund managers lining up to cheat the system in one way or another.

Her quads screamed with every step but she pushed through it, focusing on the blank, whitewashed walls and the gong of her feet on the steel. Funny how high-end hotels ignore their stairwells. The elevators were the height of luxurious design while the stairs were an industrial afterthought, a literal architectural footnote. Funneling every ounce of frustration into the onslaught, she dodged around the next corner and up the next flight. Her lungs sucked at the stale air.

The fact was that their business model invited corruption. Any hacker that could figure out a loophole through which to game their code could access the world's financial system. Any corporate executive or investor that could find a weak link in Mozaik's organization could leverage it to give unfair advantage to their own interests. She hadn't wanted to admit it even to herself but tonight had thrown their predicament into stark relief. If Maelstrom's power made them vulnerable, Mozaik's power made them vulnerable, too.

Mara rocked back on her heels as she reached the landing. Fourteenth floor. This was it. She pushed through the door and into the hall, struck again by the immediate transformation in décor. Room 391. She walked up the hall, panting.

But the minute she took off the blinders, the whole situation changed. It was no longer a catch-22 between building a successful company and bringing Lars to justice. She didn't need to balance on the razor edge of abiding by corporate best practice while sabotaging her largest shareholder. It was time to take the gloves off. And taking the gloves off meant you had to be ready to sacrifice.

Room 391. She pounded on the door with a fist. She was counting on that, actually. Someone like Lars spent his waking life orchestrating paranoid contingency after contingency. He saw her as a twisted protégé, an unwilling apprentice he could shape to his own ends. He had manipulated them so smoothly and effectively when they were trying to outsmart him for their own gain. But someone in his position saw sacrifices as offerings made in his honor. He wouldn't understand why someone would take a bullet to save another. She hoped.

She heard the chain clatter into place, and the door opened a crack.

"Mara?" An eye peeped through, disheveled hair piled above. "It's two in the morning for fuck's sake," said Vernon. "What in God's name is going on? And did you just run a marathon? You're sweating like madwoman."

"It's an emergency," said Mara. "We have a time sensitive issue with the roll-up strategy. Grab your laptop and come to Conference Room B on the second floor. Leave your phone though. Go dunk your head in some cold water and get your game face on. I need you to drag the CEOs of AMQ, Larsons, and Udemas in here for a 6 a.m. meeting. I don't care if they're kicking and screaming but they are going to fucking be here no matter what. You have my complete authority to bribe, threaten, or bludgeon them. Whatever it takes."

Vernon's eye blinked and removed the chain from its slot.

"You *are* a madwoman," he said.

Mara gave him her highest wattage smile. "Would you be working for me if I wasn't?"

40

DAVID HAD ARRANGED TO STAY in the same hotel. It was the most convenient to the string of meetings and functions that Mozaik's management team and Board were required to attend leading up to the IPO itself.

She stood in front of his door for a minute before knocking. Craig had originally introduced her to David after meeting him at a cycling shop in Boulder and geeking out over gear. Their subsequent regular walking meetings had been Mara's crash course in entrepreneurship. David never told her what to do. But he always asked her questions that made her realize things that should have been obvious in retrospect.

She smiled. James had admitted his hack of the Center for Mathematics and Society during that first meeting with David. She had been *pissed*. She vaguely remembered threatening to kick in his teeth on a curb. Ah, the joys of startups.

The bland hotel carpet and white lighting created a feel of clinical hospitality. Just standing here wasn't accomplishing anything useful. If she was going to wake him up, she might as well get on with it. She knocked on the door.

A few seconds later, David opened it and peered out at her.

"Mara?" His hair was in its usual state of gleeful disarray. He wore a gray wool sweater and navy blue sweatpants. A dog-eared science fiction paperback hung from his hand, *Hyperion* by Dan Simmons. So she hadn't woken him up after all.

"Forgive me," he said, waving her inside with the book. "Come in, come in."

They sat down in the two mildly uncomfortable chairs in the corner of the room. David crossed his legs and rested his hands on his knee.

"Of course," he said. "I'm always happy to see you." He smiled and frowned at the same time. "But my gut tells me this isn't just a social call. It's my finely honed intuition. Or maybe the fact that you're showing up at my hotel at," he glanced at the alarm clock by the bed, "two thirty in the morning. What's going on?"

Mara rubbed the rough fabric on the arm of the chair absently. "David, you've been an incredible mentor and confidante to me. If it weren't for your advice, I'd probably still be writing revision after revision of our business plan instead of actually building a company. If it weren't for your offer to lead our seed round, we very well might have given up entirely."

"You're the ones doing the real work," he said. "I'm just going on walks, eating good food, and running my mouth." He nodded. "But I appreciate the sentiment. I wish I could go back in time and give myself a few pointers. You give me the opportunity to do that vicariously."

"Given the various elephant traps we've fallen into, I'm grateful for all of those you warned us about in advance."

David chuckled. "You certainly discovered some new ones. Lars certainly tried to pull the wool over your eyes on that seed round, and I've never had a CTO test a new product by hacking other people's data."

"We've got to keep you on your toes, right?" said Mara. "Otherwise, you might get bored giving the same tips over and over."

"Mara," said David. "You have worried me, frustrated me,

surprised me, inspired me, and driven me up the wall." He tapped the side of his nose. "But I can honestly say that you and Mozaik have never, ever managed to bore me."

"Hah. Well, we do our best to keep it lively."

David raised his eyebrows as if to say, are you going to get on with it?

Mara bit her lip. "Remember when you warned me about how IPOs can fall apart in the blink of an eye? You said, 'don't fuck it up.'"

He nodded.

"Well," she scrunched up her face. "I fucked it up and the IPO is going to go sideways. You've been our biggest ally and champion since day one, and I wanted you to know first."

David looked at her for a moment. Then he stood, walked over to the minibar and poured two tumblers of scotch. He balanced them both on top of the tattered paperback on the side table between them.

"Do you know what I tell entrepreneurs not to read?" he asked.

Mara frowned and shook her head.

"Business advice books," he said. "They're the worst. Advice is horseshit. It's all anecdotal and pulls from such a tiny sliver of human experience that it has no hope of being statistically significant. Just because I went through something and think I've learned something from it doesn't mean that lesson is at all relevant to your situation. With a few rare exceptions, most business advice books are just intellectual masturbation. They're stuffed with cute tidbits of curated wisdom. The trouble is that there are a dozen books out there that will tell you the exact opposite with the same level of conviction." He waved a hand as if to swat away the entire genre. "No, entrepreneurs don't need to read business advice."

He gestured to the book on the table. "They should read science fiction, fantasy, or narrative nonfiction. They should read books that invite them to explore new worlds, imagine other realities, and think outside the box. Stories are the original form of virtual reality. They force you into extreme situations that you'll never have to face in real life. But those simulations give you metaphors to deal with uncertainty. They let you peer into other people's hearts and souls. Then you can draw your own damn conclusions. Entrepreneurs should read William Gibson, Neal Stephenson, William Hertling, Ursula Le Guin, and Andy Weir."

"I'll make sure to include them in my reading list." Mara reached for the scotch. This wasn't the reaction she had anticipated. Revealing that Mozaik's IPO might be off track a day before they were about to go effective didn't seem like a natural antecedent to speculative fiction reading recommendations. She might as well go with the flow and drink her drink. But David raised a hand to stop her.

"Not yet," he said. "First I have to tell you about Melanie Lopez."

"Who?" Mara withdrew her hand.

"Melanie Lopez was orphaned when the Nicaraguan government put her parents in front of the firing squad for political opposition to the regime. She was twelve years old. Melanie managed to cross the border into Costa Rica. She picked up odd jobs at the tourist beach hotels in Tamarindo. After pulling fourteen hour shifts, she would go to the local internet café and spend money she couldn't spare to get online and teach herself math. She ended up learning to code, too. She frequented hacker forums and figured out how to forge herself documents proving that she was a Costa Rican national with a degree in computer science from the Instituto Tecnológio. She applied and won a United Nations scholarship to study pure math at the University of Tokyo."

Sometimes Mara wondered whether David made up some of his stories out of thin air. But every time she looked up any of his tales that seemed downright impossible, they checked out. After what they had been through over the past two years, she was beginning to think that anything was possible.

David mimed a plane crossing an ocean with his hands. "While there, she learned to speak Japanese like a native. She went to Stanford for her postdoc but dropped out after she built an online marketplace for manga and anime that eclipsed all the other retailers. She had artificial intelligence algorithms coding every comic book and animated film in existence. It was a store, forum, reference guide, and discovery engine all in one. She used the proceeds to buy computing power on Silk Road, renting botnets and running distributed denial of service attacks against the Nicaraguan leadership from her apartment in Oakland. Her operations helped instigate and accelerate a regime change. She poured the rest of the money into a nonprofit that houses, clothes, and educates Nicaraguan orphans."

"She sounds like an impressive woman," said Mara. And she thought Mozaik's situation was shitty. Being victimized by your government with no opportunities or resources was a thousand times worse.

"She's a fucking ninja!" said David, his eyes popping wide open. "She's a genius with the work ethic of an ox on steroids. She had every opportunity to give up and revert to fatalism. Any decent person would have pitied her. But instead, she got her hands dirty and did something about it. She didn't know where spending every *colón* of her savings in that internet café might take her. But she always, always pushed forward. I hear you're going on *Hedrick's Report* again tomorrow. Remember that interview you did last year?"

"Sure," said Mara, thrown by the sudden change of subject.

"Last time you described yourself as *relentless*." David opened his eyes wide again. "Relentless. Words have power and that one's a doozy. You *are* relentless, Mara. You and Melanie would get along swimmingly. Or you'd murder each other with your bare hands. One or the other. You're a tornado crammed into a human body."

He leaned back and crossed his arms. "I didn't invest in you because I need more money. I've got enough money. I didn't invest in you because the market opportunity was too good to pass up. There are endless market opportunities out there. I invested in you because you have something burning inside you. I invested in you because I wanted to fan the flames and see what happened. I invested in you because I wanted to do anything I could to put wind in your sails. You didn't give me any other choice."

"Now," he reached forward and plucked up both tumblers, handing one to her. "Here's to Mozaik. Here's to James. Here's to you. You say the IPO might go sideways, that we'd flush the exit down the toilet. Well, I'm not here for the exit. I'm here for you."

They clinked the glasses together and drank. Fire coursed down Mara's throat and sent fingers all the way to her toes.

"If you fucked this up," said David. "I can only imagine it was for a good reason. If nothing else, I'm sure it will make for a compelling, albeit expensive, story." His eyes twinkled. "And if I were a betting man, I'd venture that it has something to do with that secret you wouldn't share at Taj."

41

THEY HAD TO TAKE OVER Conference Rooms A and C as well. James set up in A all by himself, headphones piping instrumental techno into his ears and Martin, the concierge, delivering a constant stream of oolong tea. Reverse engineering the code would take hours under the best of circumstances and for obvious reasons, he had no support from their team in Boulder. It was just him and the command line.

Conference Room B remained the center of operations. Greasy paper plates, discarded energy drink containers, and napkins littered the table. Multicolored scribbles turned the whiteboard in a psychedelic canvas of strategic brainstorming. Juliana started making calls at 4 a.m., lining up her network of confidantes within the US federal government, the Dutch High Tech Crime Unit, and Interpol.

But Martin had really shone on Conference Room C. Artfully arranged platters of fresh lox, red onion, capers, gourmet cream cheeses, and bagels, still warm from the oven, were interspersed with sweating carafes of fresh squeezed orange juice. Notepads, pens and paper were within easy reach and the state-of-the-art videoconferencing system was humming happily.

They would all be in there right now. It was time to go. Mara stood. Juliana looked over and nodded to her as she rattled off a bunch of operational jargon to whoever was on the other end of the line.

Mara straightened her blouse. The shower had made her look less like a junkie in need of a fix. Hopefully the combination of hot water and caffeine would carry her through the day. She traversed the carpeted hotel hallway to Conference Room A.

Slipping in, she tapped James on the shoulder. He pulled out his headphones and looked up.

"Is it time?" he asked, something flitting past beneath the surface of his eyes.

"It is." She nodded. She still couldn't believe this was happening. They had poured gallons of blood, sweat and tears into Mozaik. They had dropped out of college to make this happen. She had fought with Craig over her obsessive dedication to the startup and ultimately broken up with him when he hadn't told her he was following the trail Mozaik had uncovered. Raising the seed round had been so frustrating that she had feared she'd need to abandon the project and seek work as a barista. After TechPitch in San Diego, she had stared out over the dark water and doubted they'd ever be able to make anything of it. She never would have imagined that a few brief years later they'd be at a luxury hotel in New York City, about to ring the bell for Mozaik's Wall Street debut as America's hottest new tech darling.

"You sure you want to do this?" He pushed away his bangs. "It can't be undone and it's going to piss a lot of people off." Pissed didn't even begin to describe how people would react. They obviously wouldn't announce anything publicly until this was all over. In the meantime, they were restricting the inner circle to need-to-know and betting that the compressed timeline would preempt leaks.

"If anything, it's more your decision than mine," said Mara. "It's your baby."

Mara flashed back to their dinner in James's apartment the

night of the engagement. Danielle's concerns had turned out to be prophetic. If only they could recapture the unadulterated joy of that evening. But death rewrote all the rules.

James stared at her for a moment. The universe seemed to revolve around them, all the lights and people and madness that dominated this little rock called Earth. Then a grin flashed across his face.

"Fuck it," he said. "Babies have to grow up someday, right? We didn't do it for the money anyway."

She pulled him into a fierce hug. It was like unlocking a pressure cooker. A weight she hadn't realized was there lifted from her back. The endless effort they had driven into Mozaik. The obsessive anxiety over so many decisions. The smoldering angst born of working in close quarters on tight deadlines. All of it and more had burrowed into her heart, carving out a dark nook of fear and paranoia. CEOs might appear enviable from afar, but the reality of leadership was an intimate, no-holds-barred wrestling match between a leader and her inner demons. You had to leave everything on the field and constantly go beyond the limits of willpower. Harrowing barely began to capture it.

"Fuck it," she said into his shoulder.

After a moment they pulled back, and he angled up the screen on his laptop. He grabbed her hand and placed her index finger next to his on the enter key.

"We should do it together," he said. "We split our equity fifty-fifty after all."

A lump rose in her throat. They had agonized over that decision for ages. The argument had almost ended Mozaik before it even had a chance to get started. How insignificant it all felt in retrospect, like getting assigned a detention in middle school. It all felt like so long ago.

"If we're going to do this thing, then let's get it over with," she said.

Staring at the screen, they counted down together. "Three. Two. One."

They pressed the enter key. A small loading icon appeared on the screen.

"We're the world's oyster now," said James.

"That's it?" said Mara. "I was expecting something more dramatic."

"Like what?"

"I don't know... A standing ovation? A drum roll? A twenty-one gun salute?"

James raised his eyebrows. "The lack of pomp for a job well done is one of the reasons I've always loved building things. Quiet satisfaction is the best kind."

"And I always go for the flourish," said Mara. "Well, I guess I'm about to get more attention than I want anyway."

"Good luck," said James.

"I'll need it," said Mara. "It's going to be an unfriendly crowd."

"You seem to have a knack for finding those."

"Hey, screw you too," said Mara, punching his shoulder. "Now make this damn thing work while I go herd the cats."

42

TAKING A DEEP BREATH of recirculated hotel air, Mara reviewed her mental checklist. To hell with it. There was nothing to be gained by overthinking the situation. Best to just keep everything moving.

She pushed open the door to Conference Room C and stepped inside. Incredibly, Vernon had somehow managed to drag both Harmon Wells and Frank Von Lick to this rendezvous in person. CEOs of Udemas and AMQ, respectively. Ken Li from Larsons was piped in from San Francisco via secure videoconference on the wall projector. It was 3 a.m. on the West Coast. She made a mental note to buy Vernon a stiff drink when this was all over.

Vernon, Frank, Harmon and Ken all looked up at her as she entered. She waved them to sit and moved to the head of the table.

"Thank you all for being here," she said. "I know how unusual this is and I appreciate you respecting the urgency of the situation." She nodded to each in turn.

"Let me get right down to it," she said. "First of all, everything said here today is strictly confidential. I'm not saying that to appease our lawyers. I'm saying that because what I'm about to share has dramatic consequences for all of our businesses and you may not discuss any of the strategic implications with anyone outside of this circle until Friday. After that, you can have a field day. Are you all on board with this?"

The men nodded, shooting sidelong glances at each other.

"We need verbal confirmation," said Vernon.

"Yes," they echoed.

"Alright," said Mara. "Mozaik will not be acquiring any of your companies."

"*What?*" said Frank. He removed his glasses ran a hand over his bald pate.

"We are not buying your businesses, gentlemen," said Mara. "I know it may come as a shock."

"But we've initiated due diligence," said Harmon. "This is the deal we've been working with Vernon on for six months now. We have board approval to move forward."

"I know," said Mara. "And I apologize for the abrupt about face. But the roll-up is off the table." Harmon was fuming, his face red. Frank was tapping his pen on the table and his gaze was focused a thousand miles away. But through the jittering videoconference line, Ken just frowned and sipped his coffee.

After careful market analysis, Mara and Vernon had selected these executives and their respective firms as prime targets for Mozaik's post-IPO war chest. These men were experienced operators and ran large organizations that had served the financial industry for years. Vernon had spent most of the intervening time, between Juliana's revelation and the IPO, grooming and cultivating the deal with their management teams and boards. Acquisitions were delicate things. They were expensive, difficult to pull off, and could fall apart at any time. Even if they went smoothly, integrating teams afterwards was often a nightmare.

But it was Mozaik's only option to meet the demand sparked by the STEM Act. They had already shouldered the burden of building, improving, and maintaining a breakthrough piece of technology. Building a global scale service organization from scratch would have depressed their growth curve for years. But these three men already employed armies of skilled financial analysts and support staff. By rolling up their companies, Mozaik would be able to deploy worldwide through established channels with the level of support that banks required.

"This is ridiculous," said Harmon. "We'll sue the shit out of you for misrepresentation."

Vernon raised a hand. "Not until Friday you won't."

Coffee splashed over the lip of Harmon's mug as he raised it off the table and he hurriedly mopped it up with a napkin. "I'll do what I damn well please," he said.

"I think you'll find we've done nothing that warrants a lawsuit," said Mara. "The fact that we are informing you this early constitutes quite an act of good faith. But, as Vernon says, you are more than welcome to form your own legal opinion by consulting counsel on Friday. Any effort to do so beforehand would undermine and confuse the case you'd hope to prosecute anyway."

Frank shook his head. "You're going too far. Why are we even having this conversation in the same room at the same time? Why at six in the goddamn morning? This isn't even halfway appropriate. I've got a six-year-old to drop off at school and an 8 a.m. breakfast meeting."

He had a point. These men were competitors. Their firms offered many of the same services, and the distinctions between their business lines were niche. If they were just calling off the deal, then there was no need for this kind of full throttle get together. Vernon could simply have called each of them and relayed the disappointing news personally.

Ken raised a hand on screen. "Ms. Winkel," he said, taking another sip of coffee. Frank and Harmon perked up when he spoke. Vernon had told her that if negotiations got tough on acquisition terms, Ken was by far the savviest operator. "I assume you would not be disturbing the morning routines of these two august men without due cause. Why exactly have you assembled us this morning? No doubt there must be something beyond the regrettable demise of this acquisition spree."

Vernon raised his eyebrows as everyone's gaze snapped back to Mara. She gave a tight-lipped smile and nodded. Harmon harrumphed and Ken shot him a look that could have melted plastic.

"The reason I asked you here today," she said, ignoring Harmon, "Is because I'm offering you something more valuable than cash and stock. If you found the acquisition offers attractive, they are nothing compared to this."

Ken leaned back in his chair. Frank crossed his arms.

"And what is this too-good-to-be-true treat?" asked Ken.

Mara inhaled. This was it. "Complete transfer of Mozaik's intellectual property. Five minutes ago, we released all of our core source code to the open source community under a Creative Commons license. We will work with each of your firms exclusively for a nine-month period to get your technical teams up to speed and train your staff in best practice. During that same period, your companies will become the only officially endorsed Mozaik implementation partners. We're handing you first mover advantage for a white-fenced business line on a silver platter."

It was incredible how quickly Harmon's expression changed from self-righteous indignation to avaricious glee. "Mara, Mara," he said. "Perhaps we could have a private word about exclusivity before taking this discussion further. Udemas would be very interested in finding a way to work together as the *preferred* partner." He placed a conspiratorial emphasis on the word that made Ken shake his head in disgust.

"Hold your damn horses," said Frank. "Did you say *open source*?"

Mara nodded. Danielle had outlined it with such conviction. *The fundamental problem with computer security is that proprietary software has an inherent weakness. If your code is closed, and someone* discovers a bug, then it's easy to exploit. That's why Linux works so well. It's open source. The code is available to everyone for free. That means that thousands of people have combed through it countless times and helped each other to fix bugs and close holes. At the end of the day, any proprietary piece of code is far weaker than its open source equivalent. Armchair philosophy made real.

"But, but…" said Frank. "You're flushing twenty years of patent protection and trade secret status down the toilet. It'll turn your algorithms into a commodity. They'll be everywhere."

Mara raised her eyebrows. "Why, that's exactly our goal. Our algorithms are designed to be a part of the world's financial security infrastructure. By making them open source, we hedge against any attempts at tampering or manipulation. I think we can all agree that our financial system should not be exposed to the vagaries of collusion or criminal gambits. Releasing under Creative Commons and opening the kimono puts Mozaik's efficacy beyond dispute. Everyone can see how well it works. Everyone can improve it. Everyone can use it. It will become one of those invisible cogs and wheels that keep progress chugging away."

Harmon raised his forefinger. "About that exclusivity clause, we'd be willing to offer☒"

"Enough," said Ken. He didn't say it loudly but the effect was immediate. Tendrils of silence spiraled through the room. He cocked his head to the side, never taking his eyes off of Mara.

"Ms. Winkel," he said. "By my count, you have approximately twenty nine hours before your virtuous little company is scheduled to ring the bell on Wall Street. I believe the current estimate of your expected market capitalization is somewhere north of one billion dollars. All that value derives from a single thing, your source code. Releasing that code into the wild is like opening a bank vault, announcing it with a megaphone, and serving free lemonade as looters race away with the cash. Perhaps you would care to enlighten us as to the reasoning behind this sudden change of course?"

"Our team is committed to making the most impact we can in the race to disrupt money laundering."

"Nevertheless," said Ken. "You also bear a fiduciary responsibility to maximize shareholder value. Unless, of course, you are planning to pull your IPO entirely."

Mara gave him a look packed to the brim with innocence. "To establish a basis of good faith for our ongoing partnership, we are informing you of this strategic decision before even our bankers."

"How very thoughtful of you," said Ken.

"And we believe that strengthening our common financial well-being and excising criminals from the system is more important than simply accumulating wealth."

"No doubt," said Ken. "Your principles are beyond reproach. What a pleasant surprise to collaborate with such an ethical young leader," said Ken. "Far too many entrepreneurs these days are simply interested in the mundane pursuit of cold, hard cash."

The other faces in the room were turning back and forth between them as if following a tennis match.

"We strive to serve," said Mara. This little tête-à-tête was edging onto thin ice.

"Just one more question, Ms. Winkel," said Ken, with a wide smile. "Your offer is most generous. Indeed, you are sacrificing your company on the altar of public service. Instead of gobbling us up with your Wall Street winnings, you are handing us your beating heart. You do us far too much credit and we are, of course, deeply honored that you would consider us for such worthy mandate." Harmon looked around, confused as to who he should be honored by for what. "But please humor my base manners. I simply must ask. What do you want in return for this magnanimous gift?"

Mara smiled. This is where it got interesting. "Oh, nothing very much," she said. "We only ask that you help us with a small side project. It won't take more than a day or two."

"Ahh," said Ken, smacking his lips. "A side project. Those are always *fascinating*."

43

THE DAY WENT BY in a caffeine-fueled blur. Juliana came in to reinforce the need for secrecy with the seal of Presidential mandate, and left with a plate piled high with smoked salmon. Vernon worked out a rapid deployment roadmap that fit Udemas, Larsons, and AMQ's various corporate structures and client bases. James hosted a secure conference call with their respective technical officers to walk through the operation step-by-step and then began fielding the endless flow of logistical questions as they went live. The operation began in earnest.

Meanwhile, Mara showered and headed off for back-to-back meetings with Zach and his team of bankers. There never seemed to be fewer than fifteen people around her, and Grant and Leslie never left her side. David, Lars, and the other directors flitted in and out for discussions that required board approval or oversight. Every time Lars entered the room, Mara had to push down a panic attack. She took refuge in David's laughing eyes.

She struggled to maintain the façade of excitement and seriousness appropriate to a CEO on the day before a Wall Street debut. Everything needed to go as planned until they were ready to pull the plug. They couldn't afford to have Lars suspect anything.

Zach reviewed last minute changes to The Book but Mara's mind was elsewhere. While she tried to answer the endless stream of questions and sign the reams of paperwork that the legal team produced, she knew that the real work was going on back at the hotel.

Her focus eroded time and again and she found herself asking too many clarifying questions and trying to catch up midway through a conversation. Then she would reel herself back into the present moment, chuckle, pick up a pen, and scrawl the requisite signature. The most important thing she could do to help her team right now was to keep the charade alive, and them with it.

44

_____

THE BOARDROOM on the sixth floor of the New York Stock Exchange was an opulent cavern. The soaring ceiling was crafted from Tiffany glass, and the lush carpet was soft under Mara's shoes. Cream walls with ornate gilt columns and intricate inlays gave it the feel of a financial Versailles. An oval solid wood table that could sit more than forty people dominated the room and the original Stock Exchange clock hung over a polished podium at one end. The tuxedoed staff was laying out place settings, coffee, and fresh fruit. Thankfully she had been able to grab a few hours of restless sleep before this 5:30 a.m. breakfast.

"I've got to admit, I never thought I'd be joining my daughter for an opening bell ceremony." A big hand landed on Mara's shoulder, pulling her out of her reverie. "You look like the warrior queen of corporate America in that foxy dress."

"Dad." She turned and embraced him. His ex-football-player bulk still made her feel like a small child in his arms. They pulled back and she poked his belly. "You're looking fat. Too much sushi I see."

He laughed, teeth a flash of brilliant white against his ochre skin.

"Hey sweetie, we're all so proud of you." Mara's mom appeared and wrapped her in another hug. A high-tech hearing aid peeked out of her mom's ear, the latest attempt at mitigating the effects of the cochlear infection. Her parents had arrived together. Despite their separation, they were still on friendly terms.

Mara remembered the last time she had seen them in the same room. It had been on that fateful Thanksgiving weekend when she stormed out of Osaka in L.A. She had been so angry. But it was hard to recall why. Something about how she thought they weren't being supportive enough of Mozaik. Self-righteousness was a divisive thing. If nothing else, she hoped she'd learned to use it more sparingly.

"Thanks for coming guys," she said, and squeezed their hands. "It's really special to have you here." A lump rose in her throat. She realized that it was true, although not for the reasons they assumed.

Something tugged at the edge of her thoughts, a loose thread tossing pebbles at her bedroom window. There were so many people she wished she could share the truth with. But they just couldn't risk expanding their little circle of trust any farther than strict need-to-know. She was tempted to lean in and whisper some word of warning to them but she pushed down the urge. The whole world would know soon enough.

Over their shoulders she saw Mr. and Mrs. Chen hugging James. She smiled. Mrs. Chen had been their first customer, hiring Mozaik to vet her accounting firm's data as they prepared for tax season. They had pivoted since then. They now served banks, not accountants, and their algorithms had evolved far beyond what had been possible two years ago. But Mrs. Chen, with her sharp wit and surgical questions, had written them their first check,and had given them their first sliver of revenue.

"Ahh, these must be your parents." The voice loosed a flood of cold adrenaline through Mara and she suppressed a flinch. Her mom caught the micro expression and gave her a curious look.

She braced herself and turned to face Lars. His eyes were slate gray and as cold as ever. His spotless suit fit so perfectly that he could have graced a magazine cover. A slick, wet feeling gurgled within Mara. She tried to keep blood from rushing to her face or her voice from shaking. She only needed to keep up the act for another hour or so. At least he might write off any odd behavior as a reaction to Danielle's murder.

"Yes, they're out from California," she said, forcing a smile.

"Wonderful to meet you both," said Lars. "Pasadena right? The land of smiles and sunshine. Well, you did a great job with this one." He tipped his head to indicate Mara. "She's the most promising young executive out there today."

"We're lucky to have her," said her mom, her tone oddly neutral.

The smile her dad gave Lars as they shook hands didn't extend past his face. Her dad had been instrumental in helping them turn their initial financing round around when Lars and Dominic had tried to screw them. Her parents didn't know the extent of Lars's crimes, but they already had enough reason to dislike him.

"Family is the most important thing," said Lars. Mara shivered, thinking of the manila envelope. He was so slick, so calm. If only he knew his carefully constructed empire was unraveling beneath him. What would a man under such strict control do when all hell broke loose? How would he react when his cherished discipline disintegrated? She wanted this man behind bars. She wanted him away from her parents. "I'm so happy you could be here. It's a very, very special day."

Lars turned to Mara. "Might I have a quick word? It won't take a minute."

"Okay," she said. She almost wished she could let loose and tell him ever so calmly that her little troupe had engineered his ultimate defeat. On the other hand, she was terrified that he might have picked up some clue that all was not as it seemed.

He guided her over to the clock. Her heart rate increased with every step they took.

"Feel it," he said. Rubbing his hand along the edge of the podium.

She rested a hand on it. The wood was cool and smooth against her palm.

He sucked in a deep breath through his nose. "Here we are. Inside the very soul of capitalism," he said. "You're about to embark on a journey that will make you a goddess among mere mortals. Mozaik is a beautiful thing. I know you likely hate me right now with all the fire in your heart. But you'll come to learn that the price of power is well worth it. This is the kind of VIP club that means something. Remember this moment," he gestured back at the room full of people finding their seats at the enormous table, "you'll be able to savor it for years to come. Your initiation as a player in the only game that matters."

Lars looked at her with pride in his eyes. The expression was strangely genuine, especially since he rarely betrayed emotion in Mara's presence. This was a man Mara hated, a man she had dreamed of dispatching with her bare hands. He was responsible for the suffering of so many people. But right here, right now, Mara experienced a queer sense of pity for him. He wanted so badly for her to reciprocate his twisted offer of patronage and partnership. To him, life really was a political game and his obsessive carte blanche competitiveness had banished him to an existence of solitary, cynical, violent paranoia. And she was about to rip his house of cards right out from under him.

"Ladies and gentlemen," said Zach, clinking a spoon against a glass at the head of the table to catch everyone's attention. "We've got a packed and somewhat unusual schedule this morning. After breakfast, Mara will be heading across the street to record a live interview on a special edition of *Hedrick's Report*. Meanwhile our good friends at the Exchange will give the rest of you a tour of these facilities. Then we'll all reconvene at 9:30 a.m. to ring the opening bell."

The assembled crowd broke into applause and her dad whooped. "If there's one thing I learned from Mara during the road show," said Zach. "It was to eat immediately whenever food was served. Otherwise, we would spend all our time answering questions from pesky investors and leave with nothing but empty stomachs and moist napkins."

He winked at Mara. A knot of guilt tightened in her stomach. One of the nasty side effects of their little operation was that it screwed over people like Zach who had poured so much time and effort into their IPO. Not just him, but everyone on their team back in Boulder who were waiting, with bated breath, for Mozaik to go public.

Once, she would have written it off as an irrelevant detail but after devoting the last few years to building an organization, she was all too aware of the power of unintended consequences on other people's lives. Hopefully, they were doing the right thing. Regardless there was nothing to be done now. The train had left the station.

"As luck would have it," said Zach. "Those pesky investors made the right choice and we're thrilled to kick off Mozaik's first day on the public market. Mara brought home the bacon."

He sniffed theatrically. "Oh, and what's that?" The staff was carrying in steaming platters loaded with scrambled eggs, potatoes, pastries, stuffed tomatoes, and the obligatory bacon. "I think I smell it now, so let's dig in before it's too late."

Little did he know, it already was.

45

MARA STEPPED OUT INTO THE CLEAR, frigid New York City morning. A flock of assistants and staffers circled, herding her across the street into the glass and steel edifice where the *Hedrick's Report* crew had established their temporary studio for the broadcast. Sue had said that the producers had flown out all the original furniture to make sure the set was recreated perfectly. It was amazing what some people would do to keep up appearances.

The front of the New York Stock Exchange was blocked from public access. Gates and security personnel kept the iconic stairs empty but tourists gathered on the opposing sidewalk to snap selfies with the Exchange in the background. Today a massive banner with Mozaik's colorful logo dominated the building. The morning breeze ruffled the canvas against the Corinthian columns.

A phone vibrated in her purse. She dipped her hand in. It was the burner, not her normal phone. She pulled it out. The message was from James. He had spent the entire previous day and night in a tea-fueled hackathon reverse engineering Chad's backdoor into Mozaik. The patch that he and Danielle had already developed was only the beginning. The changes had already propagated out through Udemas, AMQ, and Larsons to their clients, representing on the order of 75 percent of major financial institutions.

She opened the text. "I'm getting some weird messages from

Gordon back in Boulder," it said. "Chad knows."

Fuck. This had always been a risk. They couldn't inform their engineering team back in Boulder of the operation for fear of anything getting leaked. But anybody could stumble across the now open source code and ring the alarm. Plus, even though Frank, Ken, and Harmon were sworn to secrecy, people within their organizations or their banking clients could unintentionally query someone at Mozaik HQ. That was just the beginning. There were countless other ways the word could get out. This operation was a sprint and their success depended on executing the plan before anyone else had time to do anything to stop them.

Mara bit the inside of her cheek. This time, they were lucky. This would only advance the timeline by about twenty minutes. She thanked James and then fired off a text to Juliana. "Do it. Now."

"Ms. Winkel." An assistant touched her shoulder. "I'm sorry but you're scheduled to be on air in fifteen. We have to get you to the dressing room."

Mara took a last look over her shoulder at the Exchange. After this little stunt, they would probably ban her for life. She still felt like there was something she had missed. A pang of anticipatory nostalgia swept through her. Excitement had been building back in Boulder for months now. So many dedicated members of her team would be confused and devastated by this drastic change of direction. Their hopes for stock option packages would be dashed, at least for the moment. It would turn their worlds upside-down and even she didn't know what life was going to look like on the other side.

Every decision made ripples that fanned out to touch everyone around her. Her only consolation was that the price of inaction would surely be even higher.

"Of course," she said, dropping the burner back into her purse. "Let's get this show on the road, shall we?"

46

MARA STARED INTO THE MASSIVE MIRROR. The makeup people had efficiently erased the deep crow's feet around her eyes, excavated her hollow eyes, and rejuvenated her gaunt face. Even her hair had been tamed in record time. The elegant black and white dress set off her skin's softer chocolate tones. Skilled hands had transformed her into the entrepreneurial ideal, an evangelist filled to the brim with vim and vigor on the brink of corporate ascendancy.

They might be able to fool the mirror and the cameras, but inside she felt more like an exhausted runner on the last leg of an ultra-marathon. Entrepreneurship required imagining whole new worlds, and then doing whatever it took to realize them. Building a business was hard enough. Most founders didn't fall victim to the tangled web of a criminal conspiracy.

"Three minutes." The stage manager had a tight blonde ponytail, a complex headset, and a matte black uniform.

Mara gave her a brief nod and then returned her attention to the mirror. This was it. She had ordered Juliana to green light the sting. Right now, hundreds of federal agents around the country were serving warrants, breaking down doors, and making surgical arrests. It was hard to imagine SWAT teams bursting into Mozaik's superhero themed conference rooms to handcuff Chad.

She sighed. If only she could have shared the news with her

team in a gentler way. It was even harder to think that just across the street agents were swarming the Exchange itself to bring in Lars. She would have liked to see that in person. Pomp and circumstance, interrupted at the last possible moment. But she was CEO and the world would demand an explanation. That's why she was here in this dressing room after all.

"...this company has grown at an unprecedented pace and is already transforming our entire financial system from the bottom up." She could hear Hedrick's introduction starting beyond the door onto the set. She could imagine his immaculate attire, his perfect composure in front of the live audience and the millions more watching from home. "The woman who teamed up with her best friend to risk it all and pursue their dreams..."

"Two minutes," said the stage manager.

Then something clicked. She had been forgetting something. She pulled out her phone, not even bothering with a burner, and dialed. Once they had decided not to include him from the start, she hadn't thought of him once. With the constant rush of activity leading up to this moment there hadn't been time for review. But despite the frustration with CyFi and the illicit donations Mozaik had mapped between Maelstrom and Senator Hartfer, Xavier deserved to know about the sting before it hit prime time.

"Mara?" She could hear the stress in his voice.

"What's wrong?" she asked.

"I'm watching SWAT teams rushing the New York Stock Exchange and I don't know why," he said. "I'm not sure which is more worrying."

"That's why I'm calling actually," said Mara, it was weird looking at herself in the mirror as she talked. "We're running a raid against Lars and Maelstrom in coordination with Juliana Estevez at the White House and the relevant agencies. I'm sorry I wasn't able to tell you earlier but we've pulled together the entire operation in the last few days, and we were worried about infosec at CyFi after the investigation into Hartfer got shut down. Turns out he's on Maelstrom's payroll. For what it's worth, I never doubted you personally."

Xavier sucked in a sharp breath. He was quiet for a moment but Mara was surprised at how quickly he recovered his composure.

"Okay," he said. "It's even more worrying that I didn't know about *that*. If that kind of op could go down without me knowing, we've got bigger problems. But that can wait. You said that Lars is the target of this raid?"

"Yes," said Mara.

"Then you've got problems too."

"What do you mean?"

"One minute." The stage manager stepped from the wings to collect Mara and frowned at the sound of commotion in the hallway beyond the door from Mara's dressing room opposite the stage entrance.

Xavier was panting, it sounded like he was running. "I've been keeping tabs on Lars ever since he got to New York, why else do you think I'm here? And your gung ho SWAT teams are chasing a golden goose. He's not in the Exchange. He left ten minutes ago through a side exit and entered a building across the street."

47

"WHAT THE HELL IS GOING ON OUT HERE?" The ponytailed stage manager stepped across the room, opened the door, and stuck her head out into the hallway. The minute the door opened, the hubbub distilled into competing yelling voices.

Then Mara jerked as the mirror in front of her instantly turned into a fractal pattern of cracks and exploded into a cloud of falling shards. Only then did the sharp report of a gunshot reach her ears. The sound was painfully loud, too big for this small dressing room.

Just like in the penthouse prison, time slowed. The phone dropped from Mara's hand as she jumped out of her chair risked throwing a glance over her shoulder. The stage manager had stumbled back a few steps to lean against the wall. She was staring down in disbelief at her stomach where a bullet had torn a ragged hole. Blood was already starting to pool as she sank down to the floor.

"Where is she?" He stood profiled in the doorway, gun in hand. He saw Mara in the opposite corner and their eyes met. His expression turned feral.

She turned and dove through the doorway to the stage wings. Another gunshot thundered behind her, and splinters showered down from above. She had to get away. She had to find someplace safe. She had to tell Juliana what was happening.

He was only a few steps behind her. She ran through the darkness of the wings and surged forward into the blinding brightness of the stage. Suddenly, the entire world was nothing but blazing lights and swooping cameras, all centered on the sprawling mid-century modern steel desk and the faux background showing Mozaik's corporate logo fluttering against the columns of the stock exchange.

"Ladies and gentlemen, I give you the relentless Mara Winkel." Hedrick's smile shone as he stepped around the desk to welcome her, his signature aquamarine bowtie dazzling under the harsh lights. The audience roared with applause.

"Get down!" she yelled as she sprinted across the stage. She tried to push him but he dodged out of her way, not understanding. "Get the fuck down!"

The applause faltered at this strange turn of events and Hedrick stared at her as if she was out of her mind as she dashed across the stage and lunged forward to duck behind the desk. She pressed her back against the drawers and tried to think of something, anything she could do.

Another gunshot. She heard a gurgling sound and then a reverberating thump as Hedrick's body landed on top of the desk. His arm splayed out and a limp hand hung over the edge right next to Mara's ear, his maimed pinkie twitching.

There was sudden silence from the crowd. Mara tried to listen over the rabid pounding of her heart. Fuck. Fuck. Fuck.

Chad knows. That's what James had texted. She hadn't thought that a few minutes could make any difference at all. She had just finished eating breakfast with Lars and everyone else in the Boardroom. The whole group was fired up for the impending IPO.

Chad must have found a way to get the news to Lars at the last minute. And if there was one thing Lars could do well, it was react quickly to tactical changes on the battlefield. Now he was standing out there on stage with a smoking gun over the body of the television host.

"Where is she?" His voice carried through the hushed room like a gong sounding amidst a group of meditators.

Mara was conscious of the absence at the small of her back. If only she had her damn gun. But Lars's men hadn't returned it to her after confiscating it at the apartment and there was no way she could have laid hands on a firearm to replace it in the middle of Manhattan over the past two days. She was just sitting here, helpless.

"I will not ask again." Another shot and a scream from somewhere in the audience.

It was only a matter of seconds until someone got over their shock and revealed her pathetic hiding place. Hedrick's hand twitched again. Another victim of her carelessness. Another innocent ghost joining the line to haunt her soul. At least she would join them all soon beyond the veil. She had never imagined dying so young. Mortality was jarring and weirdly inappropriate. Then again, everyone must feel this sense of unreality in their last few moments.

Wait a minute. The frostbite story. The missing pinkie digit. Sue had said that the production managers had moved the entire set here wholesale to prepare for this broadcast. Mara leaned forward and pulled open the drawer behind her. Her hand groped around desperately. Had they taken it out for some reason? No. There it was. She gripped the handle and pulled out the ice axe.

Murmurs gathered out in the audience. It was now or never.

In one movement she leapt up and vaulted over Hedrick's body prostrate on the surface of the desk. As her feet hit the floor on the other side, she put every ounce of willpower from every race she'd ever run into her sprint. Lars was standing in the middle of the stage in his unblemished suit, staring through the lights and cameras into the crowd beyond. His gun hung casually at his side as he waited for his words to take effect, for someone out there to direct him to her.

Millennia passed between each step. One. Two. Three. Gasps sounded from behind the brilliant wall of spotlights. Lars raised the gun and began to turn. She wound up. It was just like field hockey back in high school. Four. Five. Now.

Torquing her hips so that all her momentum funneled through her screaming shoulder muscles, she swung. She poured all of the ghosts, all of the dreams, all of the broken promises into the swing.

Lars was spinning as fast as he could to face her. The ice axe whistled through the air. She caught a fleeting glimpse of his slate gray eye before the axe buried itself into it. There was almost no resistance as it penetrated through his eyeball into his brain. With strangely clinical detachment, Mara noticed how the axe reverberated with kickback only when its tip met the inside of the back of his skull.

The sickening wet thunk was punctuated with another gunshot as Lars's hand seized. The bullet careened off a camera track. Mara twisted and ripped the axe free, tearing out Lars's nose along with an avalanche of blood, brain, and gore. She watched in shocked disbelief as he wobbled back and forth. Then he collapsed to his knees, teetered, and fell backwards onto the floor.

She looked down. The ice axe, wicked and slick with blood, hung from her slack hand. His suit and her dress were soaked through with crimson. Half his face was missing and his corpse shuddered as it settled.

She looked up into the fierce glow of the stage lights. Dozens of people stared back from their seats in the audience. Millions of people watched through the cameras set up to cover the business event of the year. Mozaik's canvas flag fluttered in the background.

She was on live fucking television. Sue was going to kill her.

48

MARA STARED INTO RED BLINKING LIGHT next to the closest camera.

"This man," she pointed the trembling axe at Lars's body, "is Lars Moeller. He was the leader of the world's largest money laundering cartel, an organization called Maelstrom."

Her voice was halting. "They clean money for drug runners, arms dealers, organized crime lords, and corrupt politicians. Once clean, they manage billions of dollars of these ill-gotten gains. They are the financial infrastructure of the criminal world and without them, black market leaders lose their primary means of legitimizing their winnings."

After she forced through a few words, she picked up steam. This is what she had come here to say, what the world needed to hear. "But they aren't satisfied with the present, Maelstrom wants to hold the future hostage as well. Just like so many big corporations, they invest in technology. They invested in Mozaik."

She pressed her lips together. "We didn't realize who or what they were at first. They presented themselves as a venture capital firm, and we were flattered by their interest. Once we discovered what they were really up to, it was already too late. They had murdered our loved ones for the crime of knowing too much and manipulated us with the constant threat of further violence."

Pressing her eyes closed, she took a deep breath. "But they

weren't just after us. They had much grander goals in mind. They bribed politicians like Senator Donald G. Hartfer of Colorado to guarantee Mozaik a monopoly. They fast tracked our IPO to accelerate deployment in every bank the world over. Then they inserted a backdoor into our code to give them root access to those banks and tagged their dirty accounts with a get-out-of-jail-free card so that our algorithms would secure their funds while ousting the schemes of their competitors. Danielle O'Neil, our Chief Architect, discovered the ploy and Maelstrom executed her here in Manhattan the night before last."

The room was absolutely still around her. "Success would have deified Maelstrom within the criminal underworld and given them unimaginable power. But we realized they had made one small slip. By tagging their own accounts for protection, they opened them up to identification, too. Over the past few days, my cofounder James successfully reverse engineered their get-out-of-jail-free-card. We released our entire body of code to the open source community so that nobody would have the leverage to pull off something like this again. Larsons, AMQ, and Udemas partnered with us to run the analysis with their entire rolodex of banking clients. The results mapped Maelstrom's entire worldwide money laundering network, including the billions of dollars in their accounts and the millions of transactions with their criminal clients and corrupt confederates."

Mara shivered as the adrenaline surge began to recede. "Juliana Estevez, the President's financial reform czar, orchestrated a raid this morning to freeze all of their international accounts and capture Maelstrom's leaders and collaborators."

She glanced down at the corpse at her feet. "Lars himself somehow managed to slip through their net. But with their arrest, we have dealt a major blow against organized crime worldwide. Maelstrom is no more and bad guys will need to find a new bank."

Looking back up at the camera, she raised her eyebrows.

"Oh, and Mozaik is withdrawing the IPO. Our code is no longer proprietary, which will have a major impact on our business model. We hope that by making it open source it earns and maintains the public trust and that today's revelations will act as a proof point of its efficacy rather than casting a shadow on its origins. Thank you."

The ice axe slipped from her hands and fell to the floor, clattering as it landed. She was shivering violently now, and at a complete loss for what to do next. And then there were men all around her holding assault rifles and Xavier was in front of her, putting a gentle hand on her forehead.

As he led her off stage through the mob of uniforms and bulletproof vests, she threw one last look at the man who had raged through her life like hellfire. Lars's body lay awkwardly in a pool of blood that spread over the floor like a blush. He was diminished, pathetic. A marionette Machiavelli severed from its strings.

49

MARA RODE HIM HARD. Sweat flowed from every pore and not even the blaring Milky Chance track could cover the rhythmic thumping of the bed frame against the wall. They were sitting upright with their legs wrapped around each other's torsos. Grabbing folds of sheet between her fingers, she thrust her hips against his, pulling him deeper and deeper inside her.

A warm buzz was coalescing in her core. Every movement, every breath added layers to the feeling. She shut everything else out of her mind. Banishing the horror of the last few days, the last few years. All that mattered was sensation. All that mattered were the sparkling trickles of energy that made every inch of her body feel like a live wire.

She gasped as he thrust from a new angle, sending a tremor through the pulsing lines. She squeezed and felt him respond. Both of them riding the wave to its peak and then building up a new rhythm as they descended into the next trough. The pace of the song accelerated, the DJ layering new loops into the track as it reached for climax.

Kicking her legs out and around, she put both hands onto his chest and pushed him down onto the bed. He grunted as his torso hit the mattress, and she twisted and writhed on top of him, in search of the tempo inside her. The buzz grew from an indiscernible background noise into a roar that drowned out all thought.

He reached forward and locked his hands around her hips, pulling her down onto him. Her fingernails dug into his pecs as she found the right cadence. They were on the same wavelength, slowly accelerating along the tightrope hanging over nirvana. Time lost its meaning. She tasted copper, smelled poppies, and saw neon star trails as she squeezed her eyes shut.

As the bassline dropped, she let loose and surged against him with complete abandon. He stiffened and bucked beneath her. The thundering buzz and tributaries of energy fused into a detonation that ignited every nerve ending in her body and sent her consciousness tumbling into the Neverland of orgasm.

An indeterminate amount of time passed. Eventually she began to emerge, bit by bit, from the hazy glow. They were both still breathing heavily, collapsed side by side on the sodden sheets. Goosebumps prickled and nipples hardened as their sweat began to cool in the hotel air conditioning.

"I don't think I've ever had sex with a tornado before," said Xavier, slapping a hand on her thigh.

"Hmm? Well, you did a good job as Kansas," said Mara. Moving as if through molasses, she rolled onto her side and propped her head up on her hand.

Xavier's short blonde hair was sticking out at all angles and turned on the pillow to look at her. She looked away after a moment and began tracing the scars on his chest with her fingers.

"Fuck to forget," he said. "I know the drill. You ever wonder why I was such a good lay?"

"I see your ego hasn't gone anywhere."

"Oh, I'm not bragging. Just stating the facts. Death and sex have a way of cropping up together. The latter is one way to feel like you're escaping the former."

"This is your pillow talk philosophy?"

"I've always found that the gutter is the best place for high-mindedness."

Pushing herself to a seated position, she let her fingers traverse his torso and play around the puckered burn scars on his leg. Remnants of another violent night. He kneaded her back, coaxing knotted muscles to loosen their grip.

"You needed this," he said.

Hearing it, she realized she had.

They were quiet for a while, listening to the music advance from track to track. The beats and loops formed a fabric around them, knitting together a sense of being out of melody and bass.

"So," she said. "What are you going to do now?"

"What do you mean?"

"Well, we essentially short circuited the investigation you've spent years building. Now that Maelstrom is in disarray, where does that leave you?"

"Hah," he said. "To be honest, I'm thinking of asking Juliana if she has any openings. If this whole mess has made one thing clear, it's that CyFi needs serious reform and may need to be gutted entirely. The fact that a corrupt politician like Hartfer had enough sources and sway to mislead our leadership and keep us off his trail is shameful. I think I'll make a project out of cleaning up the place. And I've never seen a shortage of bad guys to hunt down."

"Good," she said. "The world needs more people like you, and fewer bosses like Hartfer."

"How about you? What's next?"

The swirling world beyond the confines of this hotel room came back into sudden focus. Too many questions. Too many demands. Too many unknowns.

"Fuck if I know," she said.

He snorted.

She flopped back onto the bed and stared up at the ceiling.

Organic patterns had formed in the white plaster. Her mind's eye sketched rough shapes across them and for a moment she was staring up at puffy, whimsical clouds from a sunny park in Pasadena while the adults stood around the barbecue. But that nightmare was over. She had broken the invisible strands that paralyzed her in the recurring dream. The ghosts of Taiwanese gangsters haunted another, younger Mara. She had found new horrors to replace them. If only she could banish them as effectively.

"This was the last time," she said, without rancor.

"I know," said Xavier. The pathos in his voice surprised her. It was woven through with tenderness and regret. "In my line of work, impermanence isn't just a Buddhist abstraction, it's a way of life."

50

THE CUL-DE-SAC WAS AS QUIET AS EVER. It was still early spring, but the sun shone in a clear blue sky over Denver. Mara opened the car door to discover that the air still had a chill bite to it. This suburb had a timeless quality. The groomed lawns, minivans, and well-kept houses projected an aura of safety and stability. The world might look chaotic on the news, but our kids will stop at nothing to become honor students.

Leaning back into the car, she grabbed the bouquet from the passenger's seat. The brown paper crinkled in her hands. She closed the door and walked up the sidewalk, careful to avoid the colorful dinosaur chalk drawings etched by a local toddler.

The house stood there, as unassuming and humdrum as the others, the neatly coiled garden hose and brass address numbers belying the emotional quicksand within. A bereaved mother stripped of husband and son with eyes that were windows into heartache that went far beyond grief.

Mara walked up the path and stepped onto the threshold. The turquoise door stared down at her, daring her to ring the bell. She raised a finger, expecting the psychological troll to rear up its ugly head again and chase her from this rite so long delayed.

But to her surprise, she felt nothing. There was nothing she could do to bring back Craig or Quinn. They were forever beyond her reach in the company of Danielle, Derrick and all the others. All she had to offer was support, a helping hand. But sometimes that was exactly what was needed.

She rang the bell.

After a minute, she heard noises from inside the house and then the door burst open.

Mara's mouth dropped open in surprise. A small, harried man stood in the doorway. He had on perfectly round spectacles that gave him a distinctly bookish air and wore a colorful cardigan and khakis. A screaming infant was balanced on his hip, its red face puckered up with dismay.

The man raised his eyebrows. "Yes?" He asked slowly, giving her a tired smile. He spoke with a lilting Irish accent. "Can I help you?"

It took Mara a moment to find her voice.

"Umm," she said at last. "I'm looking for Maria?"

He looked at her blankly. "I think you may have the wrong address."

"No, no," she said quickly, doubting her own sanity. "This is the house. I went to a barbeque in the backyard a few years back."

"Wait," he said, frowning and scrunching up his face to push the glasses up his nose. "Do you mean Maria Ahlgren?"

"Yes," said Mara desperately. "Is she here?"

The man looked her up and down again, his gaze gravitating toward the bouquet.

"Oh sweetie," he said. "I'm so sorry. Did you not know? Maria sold the house to us over a year ago. She moved to Sweden to live with some extended family. Are you the one who's been leaving flowers on our doorstep this whole time?"

Mara nodded mutely. It was incredible how quickly the mind could latch onto assumptions and form attachments. She had performed this unrequited pilgrimage over and over, while Maria had been in Scandinavia the whole time. Another weight cut loose from its moorings and she felt lighter standing there on the stoop.

"Hold on," said the man, cocking his head and squinting at her. "Aren't you the one from the TV news?"

But Mara had already turned on her heels and was hurrying back to the car.

51

THIS TIME SHE DIDN'T RUN. The straps of the backpack dug into Mara's shoulders as she hiked up the path from the parking lot. A light dusting of snow caked the surrounding meadows, but the path was clear and the sun hung over the Flatirons.

Eventually her steps found a rhythm and her breathing matched it. The path wound through open fields and groves of trees as it twisted its way up the mountain. The afternoon light bathed the landscape in photogenic shades, filtering through leafless boughs and glittering off snowbanks.

These mountains were part of the reason she had fallen in love with Boulder in the first place. Growing up in L.A., she had loved the constant sunshine, but dreaded the traffic-clogged freeways that mediated her relationship with nature. A decent hike was always a day trip or more. But her first visit to Boulder had opened her eyes to living in close proximity to the mountains. Here, you could go on a trail run during your lunch break.

She unzipped her fleece. The path was gaining altitude and the hike was warming her up despite the chilly breeze. A stream cut across the path, ice clinging to the muddy banks. She jumped over the gurgling brook, stuck the landing, and continued up the hill. Overhead branches threw a labyrinth of shadows onto the hard-packed trail. She held out a hand in front of her and the same pattern dappled her arm.

These mountains had become a part of her. She had jogged here as a student, goofed off here with Craig, strategized on hikes here with David, and come here to conduct clandestine meetings with her core team during the DVG sting. Terroir impacted more than wine.

A hawk screamed and she looked up to follow its slow arc across the sky, riding thermals coming up from the plains to the east. It felt good to be back in Colorado. Ever since Juliana had revealed the STEM Act rider in D.C., it felt like her already crazy life had ramped up to totally unmanageable levels of insanity.

Billionaires. Bankers. Private jets. Breakfast at the New York Stock Exchange. The madness on *Hedrick's Report* and the endless law enforcement follow-ups afterwards. All of that felt distant and irrelevant here. The hawk screamed again and then soared out of view beyond a distant ridge.

She needed this foray to the mountains. The media hounded her every step. Every reporter from primetime TV to the lowliest of personal blogs wanted a piece of her mind. Two publishers had already reached out with book deals. Some teenager had synced together clips from the terminal episode of *Hedrick's Report* into a grisly music video meme that had tens of millions of views on YouTube. The most esteemed outlets were calling it the story of the year. In popular narrative they had transformed her from Wall Street tech debutante into twenty-first century warrior princess. And it had only been a week.

The path dipped through a copse of trees and then rose beyond to climb straight up the bare escarpment leading to her destination. She sucked in a deep breath and began the climb. Her quads burned, and sweat soaked her shirt. One foot in front of the other. She focused on the ground immediately ahead, avoiding loose rocks and slippery gravel. The straps rubbed against her shoulders.

This is where she had sprinted. Pushing herself so hard that she passed out from exhaustion at the top, collapsing onto the dirt. Hunger. A visceral ache that demanded satisfaction. That was what drove founders to do whatever it took to accomplish their mission. That's what made her relentless. But the problem with hunger was that, if you weren't careful, it would eat you alive, from the inside out.

She was panting by the time she reached the summit. Catching her breath, she half expected to see Craig appear from the trail on the other side to offer her a juicy peach. But that was then and this was now.

She walked to the eastern side of the peak and sat down, feet dangling over the edge. She let the backpack fall to the ground next to her and looked out over Boulder, suffused by the late afternoon light. The brick buildings of the university glowed as if lit from within. Students were probably suffering through one of Professor Swarson's interminable lectures on governance right now. How she had despised the truckloads of homework assigned for that course. It had always been a struggle, whether to actually do the reading, or practice for her LSAT prep classes instead.

How different things might have turned out if she had laughed off James's offer to cofound Mozaik. He had hounded her as ruthlessly as the reporters did now, and his enthusiasm for the project had been contagious. But if it wasn't that, it would have been something else.

What nips at the heels of your soul? David had asked that the day they met him for a stroll up Pearl Street. *There is something ephemeral but infinitely satisfying about starting something yourself. Your shit is on the line and you and your team are where the buck stops. If you get a kick out of that, then you end up having few other employment choices. If you've got that bug, you essentially have to start a company or get involved with startups. Otherwise your brain starts to rot and you get all bitchy and miserable.*

She laughed and the wind whipped the sound away. From this vantage point, it was impossible to imagine the alternate universe where she was a second year law student. Entrepreneurship really was an allergic reaction. When this all started she had been so sure of herself, so stubborn, so aggressive. She would react immediately without considering the spiraling impacts and externalities. She had burned bridges, fouled relationships, and fucked up again and again. Those blunders had forced her to play the long game, think through contingencies, and appreciate complexity.

Pulling a container of coconut water from the backpack, she soothed her parched throat. It was easy to look back and second-guess decisions. But using hindsight as a high horse was only useful to critics and backseat drivers. She had made countless mistakes. Those mistakes hadn't just impacted their business. They had cost people their lives. But if she were to go back in time and do it again, could she really have done anything different?

David had always said that she probably shouldn't listen to him at all. *Advice is horseshit. It's all anecdotal and pulls from such a tiny sliver of human experience that it has no hope of being statistically significant. Just because I went through something and think I've learned something from it doesn't mean that lesson is at all relevant to your situation.* Now she knew only to accept advice from those that didn't overestimate the value of its impact. It was one of life's many small ironies, those with the least sense of self-importance earned the most respect.

But that didn't make the dead any less dead. Whenever she closed her eyes, Lars's ravaged face was there waiting for her and her hand reflexively grabbed for a phantom ice axe. In the fleeting snatches of sleep she had been able to steal in the past week, nightmares hid behind every corner. The feeling deep in her gut when she first learned of Craig's death. The text with a picture of Derrick's mangled body. Quinn's last stand. Danielle's execution. Hedrick's televised murder and his ponytailed stage manager staring in shock at the bullet hole in her abdomen.

Corporate executives might flock to read Sun Tzu's *The Art of War*, but few businesses had a trajectory as blood-soaked as Mozaik's. What would she go back and tell herself on day one? Take a tactical shooting course. Consider Krav Maga training. Know that corruption goes deeper than you can imagine, so don't trust the police. Oh, and make sure to implement lean software development processes. Hah. Maybe she should accept one of those book deals after all.

Squinting down at the town below, she could pick out Mozaik's roof. A building full of people she and James had recruited. A team devoted to taking a shot at the world's financial criminals. Superhero posters. Foosball tables. Competitive enmities, budding romances, and newfound friendships. All the ugly, banal, and wonderful components of any group of humans working together. Social media might make the world look flawless, but Mozaik's day-to-day wasn't elegant or exciting. But every once and awhile, a moment of pure perfection emerged from the noise. It might pass in the blink of an eye but there were glimpses of grace when all those efforts, sacrifices, hopes, and dreams aligned.

Dreams could be funny things. She remembered the sweet juice of the peaches dribbling down their chins and she and Craig devoured them sitting right here. *Mara Winkel has attracted the enmity of strong men the world over by laying bare their insidious corruptions with unprecedented technical prowess and unmatched beauty.* She smiled. Craig had affected a deep, gravelly, movie-announcer voice for that one, eyes twinkling with mischief. Turned out he hadn't been that far off after all. Half the news channels out there were spouting some version of his speech right now.

She swiped at her cheek and realized that tears were mixing with the sweat. Taking a few breaths she tried to center herself and push down the lump her in throat. Then she opened the backpack and pulled out the colorful bouquet.

The hike had left it somewhat worse for wear, a few stems were sticking out at odd angles. She unwrapped the brown wrapping paper and raised the bouquet to her nose and inhaled deeply.

These flowers had probably been grown in a Colombian greenhouse, distributed through a warehouse in Amsterdam, and traversed most of North America, before finding their way to the little flower stand on Pearl Street with the smiling student from whom Mara had bought them. Each of them was on its own journey from seed to compost heap. Dust to dust, indeed.

Orange. Purple. Green. Red. Blue. Pink. Indigo. Each flower had its specific shape, hue, charm, and imperfection. Leaning down, she brushed her lips lightly against each one. The world was so much larger than she or anyone else could understand. Her stumbles and wrong turns had consequences far beyond what she could anticipate or imagine. But living wasn't about control. Living was about showing up, doing your best, and being there for other people.

The ghosts would never leave her. But she realized now that she never wanted them too. She was a channel for their aspirations, a medium through which they lived on. She poured every ounce of hope and fear and tenderness into each kiss.

And then she wound up with all her might and hurled them over the edge. The wind caught each flower in a surging gust of mountain air. They tumbled through the fading light in a kaleidoscopic riot of color before disappearing far below.

Xavier was right. Impermanence was a way of life. It was scary. But it was also fucking beautiful.

EPILOGUE

MARA HELD PLASTIC BAGS stuffed with Terra Thai take out in each hand. It was almost 10 p.m. already. It was going to be a very late dinner. But James had only arrived in Boulder an hour ago. After the devastation in New York, his parents had insisted that he go with them to California. He hadn't had the energy to resist and spent a week with them out there.

James hadn't called, and, whenever Mara was able to get through, their conversations were brief. She got the impression his parents were always hovering, and he was retreating into himself. That's why she was walking over to his apartment now, with mountains of Thai food. They'd finally be able to talk face to face.

Another resident held the front door to the apartment building open for her. She thanked him and took the stairs up to James's floor. His ruse had worked. By reverse engineering Chad's scheme he had sparked the cascade failure in Maelstrom's plans and revealed their entire network to Juliana and her team.

She arrived in front of his apartment and knocked, but the door swung open at her touch. It hadn't been closed all the way.

Frowning she stuck her head in. "James? Are you there?"

After a moment she pushed the door all way open and stepped inside, hitting the light switch. Nothing seemed to be out of place. A few scattered monitors and a laptop on a coffee table next to an empty tea mug. It looked just as it had when they sat on pillows and dined on James's *kinilaw*. Mara remembered him appearing at the kitchen door clutching the bottle of champagne to celebrate the engagement.

"James?" Doubt coiled inside her. What was going on? Where was he?

She walked through and checked the kitchen. Empty. Bathroom. Empty. Bedroom. Empty. Mara's breath caught in her throat as she saw the Pulp Fiction poster tacked up on the wall. *Her face says it all. Sex. Violence. Intrigue. Disdain. Style. Thank you for this. It's not completely lame.* Wait, her gaze drifted down from the poster. A piece of rolling luggage sat next to the bed. She checked the tags and confirmed that it had come in on a flight from L.A. earlier that evening. What the fuck?

As she retraced her steps and double-checked every room in the apartment, the nasty feeling in her stomach grew. Something was very wrong. Shadows in the corner of the room began to take on weight, acquiring the gravity of her doubt. Why was the door still open? If he had left on some errand, surely he would have locked it.

Her search revealed nothing and she stood in the middle of the living room, unsure what to do. Then she slapped her forehead. Why hadn't she just *called* him?

Pulling out her phone, she dialed him and waited with bated breath. But instead of his voice, she heard a phone ring from the bedroom. Dashing back, she found his phone lying abandoned on the bedside table.

She forced her breathing to slow. A panic attack wasn't going to solve anything. She needed to push back the adrenaline and nerves. She needed to think. If he wasn't here, where might he be? At the office? Probably not, it would be empty right now and even if it wasn't, she doubted James wanted to see a bunch of coworkers right now. Out at a bar drowning his sorrows? Possibly, but she had a hard time imagining him doing that either. Where else?

A light bulb went off her in head and she sighed with relief. Maybe there was a completely innocent explanation to all this. Maybe she was just overreacting. She picked up the bags of steaming food and made her way back along the hall to the stairs at the other end.

She took them two at a time all the way up. She and James had hung out on the roof dozens of times. It's where they had celebrated Mozaik's first financing by cracking beers with her dad and Jeremy. It's where she had confessed discovering Xavier's true identity and mission after dousing him with boiling oil and shooting a hole through his thigh. It's where she and James had kissed for the first and only time, derailing their friendship for months.

She burst through the door and onto the rooftop.

"James?" It took her eyes a moment to adjust to the darkness.

"Just go." It was him. A wave of relief washed through her. His voice came from across the roof.

"Where are you?" She looked around to locate the source of the sound.

"Mara, just go. Okay?"

And then her relief was overwhelmed with terror. She had found him all right. James was balancing on the waist high brick wall that formed the edge of the roof. He just stood there with his arms stretched wide, face illuminated by the glow of Boulder's lights from far below. His body trembled and swayed back and forth in the breeze.

"No!" The bags of food dropped to the ground and Mara sprinted across the rooftop. The expanse of gravel was too great. Her legs couldn't pump fast enough. She couldn't get enough oxygen.

"No!" Her entire universe receded until its only constituent was the slender boy on the edge of the roof. The boy she had pulled out of the Russian River and back into the canoe while he tried to explain the physics of water skeeters. The boy who had roped her into starting a company with him. The boy who had taken down a global cartel with a few lines of code.

"I said *go*. Don't touch me or I'll jump."

"Please. Please." Mara collapsed onto her knees on the roof behind him, chest heaving. "James, please. No more death."

His laugh lacked any hint of mirth. "No more death? That's all there is, Mara. Death. I haven't been able to sleep since it happened. Danielle's always there. When I close my eyes. When I open them. When I'm doing something. When I'm just sitting there. When people are talking to me. When I'm alone. Always."

"But—"

"We were supposed to get married this year." James continued as if he hadn't heard her. "And you know what the worst part is? I can't remember how beautiful she was. I can't remember her laugh. The only thing I can hear is the sound of them breaking her neck. The only thing I can see is the back of her head where her face was supposed to be. It's sick. It's fucking sick. We got Lars and Maelstrom. That work is done. But now I can't take it anymore."

Mara was sobbing. Tides of despair tore through her. The raw intensity of Danielle's gaze pierced through the shrouds of memory. Her frizzy brown hair. Her unselfconscious intellect. She punched the rooftop again and again and again until the blood pouring from her knuckles stained the gravel.

"I know," she said, the words lodging in her throat. "I know. His kiss tasted like Clif Bar."

"What?" asked James, his voice coming from a thousand miles away.

"Craig," she said. "That afternoon you first texted me about Mozaik. We were mountain biking up in Vail. We crashed into the mud and he kissed me. He tasted like Clif Bar."

She pushed herself to her feet, blood weeping from her ravaged hands. She stepped to the edge and hoisted herself up to stand next to James on the wall. The vertigo made her head spin. Six stories below traffic moved up and down the peaceful streets of Boulder. Laughs from a passing group of pedestrians filtered up to their dark perch on the brink of oblivion.

"Maybe you're right," she said, the wind tugging at her hair. "Maybe it is time for an ending. Fifty-fifty partners, right?"

"What?" James turned to look at her and his gaze focused for the first time, returning from another world. He was wearing a plain white t-shirt.

He frowned and shook his head. "No," he said. "No. The world needs you, Mara. You burn too bright. You put Lars in his grave. You drove Maelstrom to extinction. You've got to be there to lead Mozaik. You need to be there for your parents and everyone else."

"What?" she asked, trying to keep her balance on the narrow ledge. "Why is all of that up to me? Am I just supposed to do that alone? Pining after my poor little friend James who decided he just wasn't up for it? What kind of fucked up logic is that? You think I enjoy being the most famous murderer on the goddamn planet? You think this is *fun* for me?"

"No," he said. "That's not what I mean."

"Oh, really," she said. "Pray tell, what exactly *do* you mean then? What makes you so special that you get to jump off a building and I don't?"

Something flickered across his face but he didn't say anything.

"Because it's pretty fucking obvious," she said. "You're bailing on this party. But the only way partners bail is together. So let's fucking do this already. Ready?" Her heart was pounded like jackhammer. "One. Two— "

"No!" James held up his hands and stepped backwards onto the roof.

Mara turned and dove after him, putting all of her strength, weight, and momentum into a full body tackle. Her shoulder hit him in the solar plexus and both of them tumbled and rolled across the gravel. The impact knocked the wind out of them.

"You motherfucker," said Mara again and again. "Way to ruin a perfectly decent evening."

"Fuck you," said James. "Way to ruin a perfectly decent suicide attempt."

"At least we can agree," said Mara. "That we're both assholes."

"Two assholes in middle of a totally fucked up world."

"Ain't that the truth?"

And then they were both crying and laughing and lying on their backs next to each other. After a while their breathing returned to normal. But they didn't get up. They didn't move. They just lay there and stared through the city glow at the stars wheeling overhead.

Hours later, the gray fingers of dawn trespassed the eastern edge of the night sky. The stars dimmed and birds began to sing, flitting from their nests in search of breakfast.

Mara propped herself up on her elbows. "Come with me," she said. "I've got an idea."

They both lurched to their feet and hobbled toward the door, renewed circulation sending needles of pain through their stiff muscles. She left the untouched bags of Thai food where they lay and led the way down the stairs and out onto the sidewalk.

Boulder was quiet and peaceful. This wasn't the city that never slept. The only people out at dawn were the occasional joggers out for an early run with their dogs. They walked side by side through town as the sky grew brighter overhead. They traversed campus, with its red brick and endless footpaths. They crossed the bridge over Boulder Creek, which gurgled past beneath their feet. They passed the former Center for Mathematics and Society where a bored FBI agent smoked a lonely cigarette in front of a door covered in police tape.

When they arrived, the barista was just flipping the sign inside the door to read, "Open."

The Laughing Goat looked the same as ever. The smell of roasting coffee permeated the place. A string of lights glowed from the ceiling. Abstract paintings by local artists lined the walls. Stools lined the wooden coffee bar and small circular tables were sprinkled around the seating area.

The barista raised her eyebrows and looked at them as if they were crazy. Mara laughed as she realized how insane they must look. Bloody knuckles, haggard faces, and dirty, rumpled clothes.

"One oolong tea and one double cap extra dry," said Mara.

The barista nodded and kicked the espresso machine to life.

Mara took out her credit card but the barista waved it away. "First customers of the day," she said. "It's on me."

"Thanks," said Mara, overcome with emotion at this small kindness.

They found seats near the front and sipped their steaming drinks as they watched Boulder wake up through the front windows. Pedestrians plied the sidewalks. Delivery trucks rumbled by on the street. Pigeons fluttered in for awkward landings and toddlers trundled along in colorful little outfits.

Mara felt some of her hard-won cynicism slough away as the town came to life. In this world, you always had a choice. You could try to control everything around you through fear and discipline or stick out your neck and inspire people by trusting them. You could let others make your decisions for you or put yourself in the driver's seat and take responsibility for your actions. You could live within the confines of how the world had always worked or risk it all to build a new and different model. She took a sip and relished the earthy burn of the cappuccino. She couldn't imagine anything better.

"James," she said. "I've got a proposition for you."

"Oh yeah?" He blew on the surface of his tea.

"I know of this group of weird people here in Boulder," she said. "Not just any people, they're all part of this strange club called Mozaik."

"Okay..." He swiped his hair out of his face and quirked his mouth to the side.

"Yeah," she said. "They started this cool little company together and built this awesome product that does a pretty amazing job of sniffing out bad guys." She raised a finger. "But the thing is, they're lost. They gave away their technology instead of selling it. That totally fucked over the bad guys, which is cool, but it also fucked over their business, which isn't."

"Mmhmm." James looked at her skeptically and sipped his tea.

"So this weird little club, this company, they're adrift. It probably doesn't help that their two founders have basically been MIA for about a week, leaving them to fend for themselves in this desperate time."

"I see," said James.

"But I've got something of a special relationship with those two founders and I think we might be able to help," said Mara, polishing off the dregs of her cappuccino. "Maybe we rethink what they set out to do in the first place. Maybe we turn Mozaik into a company that supports and improves the algorithms they released to the open source community. Maybe that company also advises users and law enforcement on the most vexing schemes that their algorithms unearth. Maybe the business model won't turn it into a multibillion-dollar tech giant. But all those weird people at Mozaik might get to keep their jobs and actually contribute to making a better world. I mean, I'm just spitballing here. Just like any other idea, it probably won't survive first contact with reality. But it could be fun, right?"

"Fuck it," said James, downing the rest of his tea. "I'm in."

THE END

THANK YOU

Holy cow! It's hard to believe that *The Uncommon Series* has finally reached its ultimate destination. In the fall of 2012, I sat down at my desk in our home in San Diego, opened up a blank document in Word, and started typing. Two-and-a-half years, a few nervous breakdowns, and three books later, Mozaik's story is complete.

Even more incredible is that you are on the exact same roller coaster. Writers may pen stories but those tales only come alive in readers' imaginations. I always pictured authors locked away in a distant ivory tower, or maybe a log cabin deep in a dark forest. But the reality of writing is far more intimate. These books would never have been written if it hadn't been for the many readers who have reached out and shared what the story meant to them. Hearing from you is what gets me excited to sit down and wring a tale from my soul.

I got into startups because I saw that technology could create exponential impact. I've learned that writing is similar. Books have exponential impact because they allow ideas to scale. Now I know there's a third way to generate exponential impact: relationships. True friendships transcend what we think might be possible, what we think the world might have in store for us. That's become one of the core themes of *The Uncommon Series*. That's why I care so much about my relationship with you, dear reader.

This is especially true because I'm an indie author. No fancy PR firm, big advances, or book tours along the lines of Mara's IPO road show. All of our success so far has come from one source alone: word of mouth. It makes a huge difference every time you write a review, recommend the books to a friend, or gift them to a colleague or loved one. These things may feel insignificant, but they are the only way good books find new readers.

Thank you. Thank you for traveling alongside Mara and rooting for Mozaik. Thank you for enduring the hard lessons I've learned as a storyteller along the way. Writing takes a long time to master and I'm just taking my first few baby steps.

When I started writing *Version 1.0*, I decided to take craft seriously and work to become the best storyteller I can be. Ultimately, I hope to create characters that feel like people, worlds that just might be real, and stories that can't be put down. Books are magical. They give us a little window into someone else's soul. But Malcolm Gladwell's ten thousand hours don't accrue unless you roll up your sleeves and get to work. At a minimum, I committed to writing and publishing one million words over ten years. It's been just over a year since *Version 1.0* was published and *Exit Strategy* brings the running total to 194,402 words. Life is about the journey, and so far the writing path has been tortuous, tangled, and sublime.

I'm already hacking away at the next novel. It's evolving quickly and I'm super excited to see where it leads. It will be a new story with new characters but if you liked *The Uncommon Series*, I think you'll love it. I hope to get it into your hands by Spring 2016.

We all have a piece of Mara inside of us. I'm constantly amazed and humbled by the incredible contributions that fans of *The Uncommon Series* are making to society. You guys are the real creative rock-stars. Keep it up and pay it forward.

Cheers, Eliot

P.S. To get updates on my new books, reading recommendations, and behind-the-scenes secrets, join my author newsletter. If you love my books, this is the single best way to get or stay in touch with me. Emails are infrequent, personal, and substantive. I respond to every single note from folks on the mailing list. Sign up here:

www.eliotpeper.com

ACKNOWLEDGMENTS

Authors may write alone but books are team efforts. Many people have contributed to Mara's story in countless ways that never cease to astound.

Brad Feld, to whom this book is dedicated, took a chance on an unknown author who sent him a cold email with a suspicious attachment (the first few chapters of *Version 1.0*) and has since become a dear friend. His enthusiasm gave real weight to my dream of writing the story, which I hadn't allowed myself to take seriously. I suffered from a fear that plagues every creative person: if you don't invest much into your work, you have less to lose from failure. I've since learned that the antithesis is much closer to the truth: the more you invest in your work, the more you have to gain.

Dane McDonald and the team at FG Press crafted my first two manuscripts into top-notch books and had to put up with me the entire time. Dane also slogged through half-frozen Rocky Mountain streams, struggled with congealing cow blood, and ended up getting all the details perfect for the gorgeous and disturbing photo gracing the cover of *Exit Strategy*.

My esteemed editor, Shannon Tanner Pallone, wrestled the story into shape. Kevin Barrett Kane and Emma Christine Hall at *The Frontispiece* opened their arsenal of design skills to produce the final book you're reading right now. Josh Anon brainstormed through every narrative milestone and creative blunder. Annette Pallone dissected the manuscript with her keen copyeditor's eye. William Hertling shared his substantial insights and practical tips on life as an indie writer. Tim Erickson, Matt Blumberg, Craig Lauer, Lucas Carlson, and Jay Corrales contributed enormously with their input as beta readers.

Jason Mendelson, Tim Miller, and Paul Berberian shared war stories and helped me understand how it really feels to lead a tech company through an IPO. George Eiskamp, Danielle Morrill, Jon Belmonte, David Mandell, Andrei Soroker, and numerous other founder/CEOs added additional insights. David Cohen, Jerry Colonna, David Allison, Donna Boyer, Navid Alipour, Pascal Finnette, Ari Newman, Sarah Brown, Philippe Laval, Dorian Ferlauto, Matt Gartland, Brant Cooper, Jarrod Russell, Casey O'Toole, Chris Booth, Bob Holmen, Skye Featherstone, Sean Kelly, Franco Faraudo, Daniel Zacek, Jeff Wheeland, Mustafa Nedim Tokman, Eric Ball, Steve Pollock, Nancy Li, Pete Baston, Peter Neame, Alex White, Chris Bailey, Orr Ben-Zvy, Carmen Sutter, John Mueller, Reid Jones, James Fewtrell, Cammie Houser, Becky Thomas, Christ Dittmer, Carlos Meier, David Zweier, Stephen Richard Levine, Matt Cartagena, Ian Eck, Greg Horowitt, Victor Hwang, Ken Davenport, Joey Hinson, Emmanuel Nataf, Ricardo Fayet, Jay Zhao, Jeremiah Gardner, Justin Mares, Bill Reichert, Chris Yeh, David Brin, Patrick Vlaskovits, Michael Sacca, Andrew Chamberlain, Feliz Ventura, Carlos Espinal, Michelle Miller, Semil Shah, Ramez Naam, Sandy Grason, Keith Teare, Andrew Keen, Phil Ruggiero, Andrew Fulton, Anna Ocampo, Laura Castillo, Jeremy Shure, Geraldine DeRuiter, Jon Nastor, Eric Elkins, Mike Belsito, Eric Otterson, Eugene Wan, Sebastiaan Hooft, Katie Moran,

Dillon Kwiat, Dave Heal, William Mougayar, and Sean Wise have all been tireless champions of the books.

My parents, Karen and Erik Peper, are a source of constant support and enthusiasm. Margaret Fitzsimmons read me story after story as a kid and believed in my imagination. My sister and her boyfriend, Laura Peper and Matt Cobos, helped me understand reader psychology and how to share the story more effectively.

My best friend and brilliant wife, Drea Castillo, was my true north during the thousands of trials and tribulations that went into *Exit Strategy*. She asked the hard questions and showed me new perspectives I had never considered. Nothing is more critical to creative work than loved ones who support and inspire. Claire, our painfully cute sheepadoodle puppy was my constant companion.

Lastly and most importantly, thank *you*. Readers give life to stories. Without you, *The Uncommon Series* does nothing but collect dust. Thank you for stepping into Mara's world and for sticking with her to the end.

Cheers, Eliot

ABOUT THE AUTHOR

Eliot lives in Oakland, CA with his wife and dog. When he's not writing, he works with entrepreneurs and investors to build new technology businesses as a drop-in operator and adviser. He was an Entrepreneur-in-Residence at a venture capital firm where he accelerated portfolio companies, sourced/vetted deals, and advised foreign governments on innovation policy and capital formation. He has been a founder and early employee at multiple startups. He reads books, climbs rocks, surfs waves, and travels the world.

To find out more, visit his blog (www.eliotpeper.com). You can stay in touch via his author newsletter, Facebook (www.facebook.com/eliotpeper), and Twitter (@eliotpeper).

ABOUT THE FRONTISPIECE

The Frontispiece is a creative design agency dedicated to providing professional publishing solutions to a wide variety of different clients. No matter if you are a self-publishing author or a seasoned publishing house, we are here to see your project through to the finish line.

If you are looking for intelligent solutions for your book project, please visit us at thefrontispiece.com.

Made in the USA
Charleston, SC
29 July 2015